SPOTTSWOOD POLES

A Novel

www.mascotbooks.com

SPOTTSWOOD POLES: A BASEBALL AND AMERICAN LEGEND

For more information, please contact:
Mascot Books
620 Herndon Parkway, Suite 320
Herndon, VA 20170
info@mascotbooks.com

Library of Congress Control Number: 2021913201

CPSIA Code: PRV0222A
ISBN-13: 978-1-63755-066-3

Printed in the United States

TO SPOTTSWOOD POLES
and everyone who has dreamed the impossible
so that it would be possible for those who follow.

A NOVEL

SPOTTSWOOD POLES

A BASEBALL AND AMERICAN LEGEND

WAYDE BYARD

FOREWORD BY LARRY LESTER, NEGRO LEAGUE BASEBALL HISTORIAN

FOREWORD

AS A STUDENT OF AFRICAN AMERICAN HISTORY in general and Negro league baseball in part, I found this fictional journey about a relatively unknown ballplayer during the days following Reconstruction, World War I, and beyond to be a scintillating and fascinating read. The former *Winchester Star* journalist, now educator Wayde Byard, a transplanted New York Giants and Yankees fan, provides us with a time travel Doc Brown's DeLorean could only imagine.

The principal voice of this historic travel is the athletic Spottswood Poles from Winchester, Virginia, in the Shenandoah Valley, known for its affiliation with the Civil War. Poles's tour guide and life coach is Major Holmes Conrad, an ex-Confederate officer with silver-streaked chestnut hair and a Sam Elliott mustache who did not see young Poles as a lost cause.

Before African Americans had to avoid the choke hold, Spottswood's mom, Lucy, preached to him on how to avoid the rope. Major Conrad wanted to send Poles to school. But his mom thought she knew best. Education would give her young son a desire for a better life, but in the process create an angry man full of empty ambition. Given the period of oppression, people belonging to minority groups were often taught to never speak out and remain docile and uneducated to avoid confrontations. Lucy foresaw Spottswood's future as a house servant.

As we learn from Byard, anyone can chop wood, but not everyone can hit a baseball. With a second-hand arsenal of baseball gear, Poles became an ambush hitter, attacking baseballs and stealing bases. For teammates, he ran the bases with an excitement that flushed their faces and filled their feet with pitter-patter in the dugout.

Fans were so aware of his speed in the outfield, they would not spit tobacco, swallow, or dare to blink when Spotts chased and caught dingers from foul pole to foul pole for another long out. He sprinted the outfield like air escaping from a balloon, covering the turf like the morning dew.

His reputation as a phenom got the attention of the New York Elite Giants and its manager, Moses Fleetwood Walker. Not able to read or write, Lucy signed her mark of approval for Spotts to play professional baseball in the Big Apple. The Polo Grounds became Spottswood's new homestead.

Despite Moses Walker's initial displeasure with the "field hand" from Virginia, Poles eventually learns how to hit the curveball with a commandment from this Moses. In the process, Poles meets another curvaceous challenge by the name of Emma Dixon, the daughter of a haberdashery owner, who can read and write. With illiterate thoughts about romancing, Major Conrad provided his star athlete with some Valentine's Day ideas in the pursuit of happiness. Poles would eventually hit for the cycle, learning to read, write, dress up, and waltz into her heart. Byard's account of the chase and capture of the diva Dixon is worth the price of admission.

From here, *Spottswood Poles: A Baseball and American Legend* takes us on a journey of war and peace with several historical figures. Byard sprinkles in factual tidbits about educator Booker T. Washington, Pan-Africanist W.E.B. Du Bois, political activist Marcus Garvey, writer Damon Runyon, cyclist Major Taylor, Olympian Jim Thorpe, composer John Philip Sousa, actress Mary Pickford, General George S. "Blood and Guts" Patton Jr., and the multitalented Paul Robeson. Also joining the journey are entertainers like Bing Crosby, Bob Hope, and Fats Domino. Ballers like Bill Veeck, John McGraw, Ty Cobb, Christy Mathewson, Oscar Charleston, Louis Santop, Satchel Paige, and Cool Papa Bell provide substance throughout the narrative. In the process, Byard tells a story of the provocative racial imbalance in America using sports, warfare, and politics as a crystal-clear lens, bouncing back and forth over the Mason-Dixon line with flashbacks as in a rearview mirror. Our racially prejudiced America liked nobody, not even Will Rogers.

The real-life Poles achieved the rank of sergeant during his stint with the 93rd Division of the 369th Infantry Regiment, better known as the Harlem Hell Fighters or the Black Rattlers. Originally the 15th Infantry Regiment of the New York National Guard, the regiment was federalized and redesignated as the 369th Infantry in March 1918. When Poles and the 15th Infantry departed New York City for Europe, organizers barred them from a farewell parade with other National Guard Units, some of whom made up Colonel Douglas MacArthur's 42nd Rainbow Division. The Black Rattlers were told, "Black is not a color in the rainbow."

The official record shows that Poles fought in the battles and campaigns at Château-Thierry, Belleau Woods, Champagne-Marne, and Meuse-Argonne. In December 1918, the Harlem Hell Fighters were relieved of duty and returned to New York City for a hero's welcome as they marched seven miles from Washington Square Park to their Armory in Harlem at 2366 Fifth Avenue. The diminutive five-foot-four, 117-pound (according to his military registration card) Poles earned five battlefield stars and a Purple Heart for his European service.

On both sides of the military ledger, Poles's baseball career saw action with the top independent Black teams in the country, such as the Harrisburg Giants, Hilldale Club, Philadelphia Giants, New York Lincoln Giants and Lincoln Stars, the Brooklyn Royal Giants, and the Atlantic City Bacharach Giants.

For the early part of the twentieth century, Spottswood Poles earned his place on the Mount Rushmore of ebony athletes like Jesse Owens, Jack Johnson, and Major Taylor. His post-career accolades included a notice in the *Pittsburgh Courier*, March 8, 1930, when heralded manager and scout William "Dizzy" Dismukes, whose baseball career spanned six decades, named his top nine outfielders of all-time.

Later in 1952, the *Courier's* fan survey of the greatest all-time Negro League players named Spotts Poles to the fourth team. Noted Sabermetrics creator and stats guru Bill James ranked Poles as the "best player in Black baseball" in 1915 and 1916 and the fourth best centerfielder of all-time behind Hall-of-Famers Oscar Charleston, James "Cool Papa" Bell, and Cristóbal Torriente. Twenty years ago, in 2000, *Sports Illustrated* selected Spotts Poles as the thirty-fourth greatest sports star in Virginia in its "50 Greatest Sports Figures from Each State" section.

Along with a host of skillful credentials comparable to the Georgia Peach, a serious conversation about Poles's induction into the National Baseball Hall of Fame in Cooperstown should be mandatory. The statistical evidence of his talents is now documented.

If hits could be counted as votes, Poles would be an automatic inductee. The Cobbish-like player led the 1910-1911 and 1913 Cuban Winter Leagues, the 1914 and 1916 Florida Winter leagues, and the 1920-1921 California Winter League in several offensive categories. Always among the league leaders and highly desired by the top independent Black teams, Spottswood Poles made the final ballot of 39 nominees in the special 2006 Negro Leagues Committee formed by the National Baseball Hall of Fame and Museum. Regretfully, Poles was not among the seventeen selectees.

The warrior, athlete, and business entrepreneur died in September 1962, before Dr. Martin Luther King Jr.'s March on Washington in 1963, and is buried in Arlington National Cemetery, section 42, site 2324. Like so many, Sergeant Poles never got to experience King's dream, but a bronze plaque in Cooperstown is the most fitting recognition toward that visionary prominence.

LARRY LESTER

Larry Lester is cofounder of the Negro Leagues Baseball Museum (NLBM) in Kansas City, Missouri, and served as its research director and treasurer for five years (1991-1995). Lester acquired rare artifacts from the families of Satchel Paige, Oscar Charleston, Josh Gibson, Archie Ware, Chet Brewer, and others for the NLBM's archives. The museum's current static exhibition and informational kiosks were developed from Lester's personal collection of historic photographs, accompanied by captions written from his archival news clippings. He left the NLBM in 1995 to launch NoirTech Research, Inc., combining his expertise in research and technology to strategically track the African American experience in sports and entertainment. As a dedicated advocate for equal rights, Lester actively campaigns for retroactive pensions for worthy Negro League veterans and raises funds to purchase headstones for the unmarked graves of athletes. Lester's familiar relationship with former players inspired an invitation from President Barack Obama in August of 2013 for a meet and greet with the Commander-in-Chief. Lester is chairman of the Society for American Baseball Research's (SABR) Negro Leagues Committee, which annually hosts the Jerry Malloy Negro League Conference. Since 1998, this has been the only academic symposium dedicated exclusively to the examination and promotion of Black baseball history.

Chapter One

FAMILY OBLIGATION

IT IS OUT OF SYNC.

That is the first thing that strikes George.

Looking ahead, he can see the silver moonlight of a clear Virginia night flickering between the slats of the boxcar. The light brightens and dims with the passing of trees and clouds. Beneath him, George feels the clicking of steel wheels over railroad tracks, rhythmic, with the exception of the odd loose spike.

The clicking of the wheels distracts him from what is directly beneath him. He can feel the coldness of the metal coffin, but where else can he sit? He has heard of Uncle Tazewell since the earliest days of his childhood in California—including his gallant death in Pickett's Charge. Now he is tangible, beneath him. George is glad the coffin is firmly sealed. Despite thirty-six years beneath the soil of Baltimore, it is in good condition, absent the dirt that clings stubbornly to it. It is prepared with the idea that it will be resurrected and buried again. George silently praises the foresight of the undertaker, though he seriously doubts that unnamed servant of the dead envisions a "temporary" internment of more than three decades. The military is all George's family knows—that and the duty to perform one's familial obligations.

His father is unable to fulfill this one.

George will.

The turning of the new century in a few months means the past—and all the harsh memories it invokes—should be permanently laid to rest.

George feels the train slow, then stop with a lurch. He grabs the gray military cap before it can fly from his head and straightens the line of the brass buttons on his uniform tunic. Although not a soldier yet, he will let those who wait outside see what a West Point cadet looks like: spit-and-polish perfect, even under bizarre circumstances. He steadies himself as the train rocks back and forth for a moment, locks his legs, then straightens his back into a rigid state of attention.

Outside, the intermittent light of the moon is replaced by the steady glow of torchlight.

Winchester is no stranger to the comings and goings of war. It changed hands seventy-two times—an unofficial record no one wishes to dispute—between 1861 and 1865. The tumult is gone, but the memories, both living and dead, echo.

On this night, singular torches appear on side streets, merging into a river of warm light as they make their way down Water Street to the new train depot. A harbinger of promised commerce, the stone edifice stands out among the hollowed-out ruins that still make up much of the town.

A small shadow has joined the periphery of the procession as it passes a large home at Water Street's midpoint. Spottswood Poles is doing what twelve-year-old boys do, but shouldn't. He's heard whispered preparations throughout the evening and can't resist sneaking out the back door when the heavy oak door at the front of the house closes at a late hour. Small and lithe, his dark brown skin is set off by a fine white high-collared shirt with a blue bow. His blue breeches end at the knee with white socks covering the remainder of his legs. He leaves his fine shoes beneath his bed, reckoning his worn work shoes will be less likely to make noise against the cobblestones covering Winchester's main streets. Spottswood's movements are spare, quick, lest he disturb the silence of the shadows and draw attention to himself.

Daring to get closer to the procession than he should, Spottswood creeps beneath a wagon at the end of the train depot. In front of him, a lean brigade of aging men, their features sunken by age and the inconsistent light, form in rough order in front of the train. Looking through the spokes of a wheel, Spottswood can see the head of his household, Major Holmes Conrad, approach the boxcar. He wears a dark cloak that makes his usually lean frame look bulky.

Well into middle age, Major Conrad still projects a muscular sense of command. His distinguished mane of chestnut hair is streaked with silver, and a large mustache dominates a face still handsome, though no longer youthful. After casting a glance at his surroundings, Major Conrad removes the cloak and hands it to a subordinate, revealing the uniform of a Confederate officer: gold buttons glisten in two rows down the tunic and gold braid rests on the shoulders. Before disposing of the cloak, he pulls from its recesses a hat with a fine yellow plume, which he places firmly on his head. Following his lead, the men shed outerwear revealing uniforms of varying quality, some straining to hold the girth of those that wear them, others falling loosely about bodies shrunken by age.

Spottswood doesn't know what he is witnessing, just as he knows he shouldn't be witnessing it. Still, his muscles refuse to move, even as they tingle with nervous anticipation.

The boxcar's door slides open with a creaking sound followed by a concussive bang as it hits its terminus, revealing George and his macabre cargo.

Major Conrad steps forward and speaks in a deep, authoritative voice.

"Young Patton?"

George nods his assent.

"Major Holmes Conrad. Having served with both your grandfather and his brother, I'm honored, at long last, to reunite them. The 3rd Virginia will help bear your burden."

George offers a stiff salute, which Major Conrad casually returns, as an officer would his junior in age and rank.

As six men move to the open boxcar door, roughly in unison, and lift the coffin, Spottswood watches the legs and coffin through the wagon spokes. Almost reflexively, Spottswood moves behind a barrel to get a better view, his eyes, like everyone else's, focused on the coffin. He's never seen a coffin before, at least not in use. The coffin is carried to a waiting wagon and covered with a Confederate flag. Men form ranks behind the wagon, Major Conrad and George at their head.

In front of Spottswood's hiding place, flagpoles are unsheathed, revealing the Stars and Bars and regimental colors; flags tattered from battle obscure his view. The material of the flags is thin, and torchlight shines through, making the stars gleam. Muffled drums beat a slow cadence, and the flagpoles are snapped into the air, the aged material floating as would curtains before open windows as a storm wind blows.

"Burial detail, forward." Major Conrad's words reverberate off the stone walls and cobblestones. The small unit begins marching.

The parade of Confederate veterans moves past buildings destroyed by war. Torchlight casts bizarre shadows through gaping holes in crumbling brick walls. Spottswood's shadow, unnoticed, runs across the proscenium created by one of the holes.

The horses' hooves and wagon wheels click against the cobblestones, adding to the muffled cadence of the drums. Spottswood runs toward what everyone knows is at the end of this road, a sign— Stonewall Cemetery, Dedicated to Those Who Died for Virginia.

A fine stone gatehouse, made of native limestone, marks the entrance to the cemetery. Spottswood often thinks of it as a castle from *Arabian Nights*, a book Major Conrad reads to him often. In later years, Spottswood often wonders why a poor people, barely able to keep body and soul together, would build such an impressive edifice to guard those beyond guarding, who could not appreciate its stately grandeur. But on this night, such thoughts are decades into the future.

The procession passes through the gatehouse's arch. As it does, Spottswood works his way over the wrought-iron fence that surrounds the cemetery. After a brief time, the drums and wagon noises cease.

Spottswood hides at the base of an angel monument, its arms stretched over him. The graves of Confederate troops are arranged in long ranks before him. The statue's white face glows in the moonlight, and its marble wings look ready to take flight. Spottswood doesn't notice a shadow engulfing him. Strong hands jutting from tattered gray sleeves grab him. The yellow braid on the sleeves marks their owner as a sergeant.

Spottswood starts to scream but thinks better of it. The only man who might answer the cry, Major Conrad, is ahead in the darkness, his allegiances in this matter unknown.

Sergeant George Washington Kurtz, a beefy man with a large mustache, drags Spottswood, struggling mightily, through the ranks of men gathered around an open grave. Spottswood aims blows at his captor only to see them fall woefully short.

Kurtz's booming voice cuts through the solemn silence.

"Sir, I caught this little nigger . . ."

Major Conrad raises his hand, palm open, to Kurtz.

"I detest that word."

"I found this . . . *him* watching us."

"He's a member of my household, Spottswood Poles, Lucy's son." At these words, Spottswood feels Kurtz release him, but his body feels no relief. His heart pounds, and he struggles reflexively to catch his breath. Major Conrad lowers himself to a knee in front of the boy, the intense look in his eyes more powerful than Kurtz's grip. "What are you doing here? Problem at the house?"

Spottswood thinks for a moment, but not a long one, as he feels eyes staring at him, eyes that create a palpable feeling of hatred and malice.

"No, sir. I followed you."

"He shouldn't—"

The former sergeant's words are cut off by another raised hand from Major Conrad. There is murmuring in the ranks. It ceases as Major Conrad rises to his feet and casts a disapproving gaze.

What follows is silence. Spottswood would later think this is what eternity must sound like.

"Would you have him lie?"

Major Conrad once again kneels down to Spottswood's level.

"You can go home, unless you want hold a lantern."

A lantern presses into Spottswood's hands, and he clings to it as if to life itself. Major Conrad opens the lantern's glass door, lights its wick with a wooden match, and closes the door firmly. Looking about in the glow of the lanterns light, Spottswood thinks he would prefer darkness.

The men gather around the open grave, Spottswood and Major Conrad closest to its edge. A large tombstone at the grave's head reads "THE BROTHERS PATTON."

Spottswood draws close to Major Conrad but is gently pushed to an arm's length. The men attempt to place the coffin, which has been moved from the wagon with no small effort, in its new resting place. It won't fit.

Gingerly, it is withdrawn, with whispering among the ranks— ghostly whispers. To a young imagination, it is hard to tell where the voices of the living end and those of the dead begin.

The metal coffin is far larger than the plain wooden one that has long awaited its arrival.

Before anyone can take careful measure of the situation, George grabs a shovel and jumps into the grave. He digs recklessly until striking a piece of rotted wood, which splinters.

"I need light."

Spottswood feels his feet moving involuntarily forward, drawn by the commanding nature of George's voice. Spottswood holds the lantern closer to the grave's edge. George looks up; their eyes lock. George nods in recognition.

Looking down through the splintered coffin, Spottswood sees the body of a Confederate colonel, long beard and hair, his face shriveled, epaulets visible on his shoulders.

Major Conrad pulls Spottswood back and moves past him, lowering himself into the grave. Taking the shovel from George, he uses several strong, deliberate strokes to remove a large amount of dirt. He does what he can to rearrange the fragments of the wooden coffin. He signals for his cloak to be lowered and wedges it into the hole around his dead comrade's head.

Steering it deftly, Major Conrad guides the metal coffin until it is wedged into place. He returns to the grave's rim, removes his hat and bows his head, the yellow plume beside Spottswood's face. Spottswood fixes his gaze on the plume to avoid the temptation of looking down.

Major Conrad's voice cuts through the darkness.

"Bless, our Lord, the brothers Patton, separated by death, joined in death until the time you see fit to resurrect all worthy souls. Amen."

An "amen" resounds through the darkness and the company dissolves, not in military order, but as spirits rejoining the anonymity of the night. A few men remain to complete the burial, dirt thumping on the lid of the metal coffin. The sound seems to chase Spottswood as he leaves the cemetery. If not for the presence of Major Conrad, he would be running.

Spottswood feels dread as they walk back to the large house on Water Street. He and Major Conrad lead, George following. What's behind him is done. What's ahead is unpleasant in its certainty.

The house has been home to the Conrad family since shortly after the Revolution. Built by Major Conrad's great-grandfather, Watson Conrad, it sits strategically across the street from the Market House, center of Winchester's commerce—what is left of it, at least, since the war. Apples, the local crop of choice; livestock; and dry goods of all kinds move through the ramshackle building, which has been expanded over time to house various endeavors.

Water Street takes its name from the stream that once ran beside it that now has been turned into a small canal called Town Run. Heavy downpours reinvigorate the dry stream bed that has been cobblestoned, and the thoroughfare lives up to its name.

Conrad House is above the water, situated on a small hill. At its front is a limestone retaining wall interrupted by an impressive staircase leading to a massive oaken door at the front of the three-story edifice. Built to hold a large family and several servants, Conrad House presently has but four inhabitants. The yellow paint peels a bit from the bricks, and the windows hold antique glass of the uneven clarity used in colonial times.

The roof, sections of which can open to relieve the heat, leaks.

Still, at a glance, the house appears to be the type that would welcome distinguished visitors, which it has. George Washington slept there. Other than Mount Vernon, Washington lived longer in Winchester—for twelve years—than anywhere else. He visited Winchester, then America's Western frontier, several times during his presidency. The George Washington that Watson Conrad knew was a far different man than the one whose marble likeness dots America—North and South—at the turn of the twentieth century. With flowing red hair and a temper to match, young Washington was known as a menace to friend and foe. He fought off raids by Native Americans but started hostilities with the French by raiding a nearby trading post. It's rumored that Watson Conrad freely distributed a large amount of rum to secure Washington's first election to the House of Burgesses.

Robert E. Lee slept at Conrad House before the Battle of Stephenson's Depot. A metal hitching post on the street in front of the home notes that Lee's famed horse, Traveler, was tethered there. No one uses it out of respect.

It is not the house's history but his immediate future that concerns Spottswood as he climbs the stairs. No sooner has the front door opened than his feeling is justified.

At first, the parlor appears as it always does. Candles cast a warm glow over the high-ceilinged room, unable to mask its general shabbiness. Patterned wallpaper, once elegant, now stained and pealing at the edges, adorns the walls. At the center of the main wall are portraits of Thomas Jefferson, George Washington, and Robert E. Lee displayed almost as the Holy Trinity.

Major Conrad pushes the door open—Spottswood cannot remember it ever being locked—before it is pulled back forcefully by Spottswood's mother, Lucy. An uncommonly beautiful woman easing into graceful middle age, Lucy's large brown eyes are alarmed and the tone of her voice near panic.

"Major Conrad . . ."

"It's all right, Lucy. Small boys will be curious."

"And dead if they follow that curiosity."

"Nothing so dramatic happened."

"I worry—"

"—as do I."

Before Lucy can speak again, Major Conrad raises his hand and directs her attention to George.

"Young Mr. Patton needs a warm bed. I trust you'll find something appropriate."

"We can't just—"

"—I trust you'll find something appropriate."

Lucy acknowledges her visitor for the first time, resuming the role of servant rather than lady of the house. She curtsies to George, her head bowed.

"Excuse my manners, sir. Come with me. And Spottswood—"

"—the boy and I must talk."

Another figure appears from an interior room. Tom, Major Conrad's son, is an uncommonly handsome youth in his late teens. His young features are at odds with his dress: black pants, a white shirt, a black bow tie, and black vest. It's the uniform of a serious student. Spottswood cannot remember a time when Tom wasn't a man of consequence in training.

"Anything I can help you with?" Tom is always helpful.

"Not at this time," his father replies.

"If a servant in our home is—"

"—Not at this time."

Tom, a look of annoyance on his face, retreats. Spottswood notes that Tom habitually appears at inopportune times and vanishes when no opportunity presents itself.

Lucy and George disappear up a staircase with Lucy shooting daggers over her shoulder at Spottswood. Major Conrad goes through a door leading to the kitchen at the back of the house, Spottswood trailing behind him as if pulled by a magnetic force. Before he reaches the top step, George turns and speaks to no one in particular, his eyes glassy. "That is the only time I saw my grandfather."

The kitchen is clean, not elaborate. The china on the shelves has suffered some casualties in its chipped ranks. A dim oil lamp illuminates the room.

Major Conrad turns up the wick in the lamp, increasing the illumination. He searches the back of a cabinet until he finds a bottle of whiskey. He works the sink pump to pour a glass of water, which he places on the table in front of Spottswood before pouring his own drink and sitting down.

"Sit down, Spottswood; servants are not required to stand in our home. Besides, men should sit comfortably when having a drink."

Spottswood sits awkwardly, studying the glass before him, running his fingers nervously over its exterior.

"Do you know what you saw tonight?"

"A dead man."

"I imagine you'll be seeing him for quite some time. I still see them. What else?"

"Can't get past the dead man."

"He was much scarier in life than he was tonight. His name was Colonel George Patton from Parkersburg. That's located in what they now call West Virginia, but there was no greater lover of our commonwealth than George Patton. He was wounded in Third Winchester at Hackwood Park on what was our left flank. That was the day your mother was born."

"She was born during a battle?"

"In the summer kitchen downstairs. Her father, Ezekiel, and my father went to raise a section of the roof to relieve the heat; it was an uncommonly hot day for mid-September. Some Federals from Ohio were on the hill where Mount Hebron cemetery is now. They thought poor Ezekiel and my father were artillery spotters for our army and let forth a fearsome volley. You can still see the bullet pockmarks on the upper story."

"Were they killed?"

"No. Ohioans are notoriously poor shots. They make up for that with their oratorical skills. Several have been elected president, including William McKinley, our current president. He was a mess sergeant when his unit fought here."

"The dead man . . ."

"Colonel Patton. Old Phil Sheridan came storming down the pike from Berryville and knocked us flying back through town. Not that we weren't outnumbered . . ."

"Three to one."

"I've told this tale?"

"Not about my mother. Not about the dead man."

"You do not lose the thread of the narrative I'm weaving, despite my meandering. Lawyers do that." Major Conrad takes a long sip of his drink. "Our line broke before a fearsome cavalry charge; some say the largest since the days of ancient Rome. We started retreating, a fearful tangle of horses, men, wagons, and cannon. Colonel Patton stopped his horse and told us what cowards we were—how we should turn and face the enemy."

"Did you?"

"No sooner had he said this than a shell hit at his side. Killed his horse and splintered his right leg. Since I was an officer, they brought him here, laid him in our parlor. The surgeon was called, Doctor McGuire, the same man who took Stonewall Jackson's left arm at Chancellorsville. Colonel Patton lay there with a pistol across his lap—huge horse pistol—saying they wouldn't take his leg. He had survived such a wound at Sharpsburg and swore he'd survive again. By the time they got the gun away, infection had set in."

"He died."

Major Conrad drains his glass as he nods assent.

"I have the pistol and the colonel's saber somewhere. I shall have to give them to the boy."

Spottswood takes a drink.

"Who was in the coffin from the train?"

"Colonel Patton's brother, Tazewell, killed at Gettysburg in Pickett's Charge. The Pattons have a flair for dramatic exits. The young gentleman upstairs is Colonel George Patton's grandson, also George, who seems to have inherited the family's temper, God save him. He is a cadet at West Point soon to join his family in California. He had to close this chapter of his family's history. Is there anything else you'd like to know?"

"No, sir."

"That said, Spottswood, your mother is right. Don't undertake such an adventure again. There are people, bitter people, looking for someone at whom to direct their rage. Coloreds, unfortunately, are a target for such people. Don't be afraid of them, but don't act in a way that would make you a target. I don't know how I would live here without you to shield me from your mother's wrath."

Major Conrad pours a second glass of whiskey and clinks Spottswood's glass. Spottswood detects a wink in the flickering light.

"Not a word to your mother."

Chapter Two

THE DEVIL'S GAME

LUCY IS A PIOUS SOUL, but church bores Spottswood. The preacher talks about suffering almost constantly. Moses and his wanderings in the desert are a favorite subject. The singing is boisterous and beautiful but ends too quickly. Sitting through the sermon is too much for a body perpetually in motion. The food afterward is always good, but after a few mouthfuls, what is there to stay for?

Spottswood sneaks away from a church social and begins working his way through back alleys. His green velvet suit is designed for a young gentleman not engaged in the sort of activity Spottswood favors on his day of rest. Barking dogs and the sounds of broken glass underfoot replace the pleasant conversation of the church. Spottswood passes discarded furniture and splashes small puddles of standing water. At length, he places his hand beneath a section of fallen fence to retrieve a weathered baseball bat. He begins playing baseball at the age of six, competing with older boys after church. His talent soon has Spottswood competing against much older foes with more than good-natured bragging rights on the line.

The bat is a gift from a church elder. The Federals brought

baseball from New England with them. African Americans around Winchester adopted the game as an act of defiance. Whites picked it up when they found, much to their annoyance, that it is fun and that they have an aptitude for it.

Spottswood's bat looks as though it is Union Army surplus: a reddish hickory stick hardened almost to the consistency of stone by age. At first too large for him to handle effectively, Spottswood learned to choke up on its thick handle and bunt using his blazing speed before he learns to slap the ball to all fields with exceptional effectiveness.

The bat retrieved, he passes white children playing baseball on a small pasture, the game moving slowly, politely. At Spottswood's destination, such civility does not exist.

The "secret" sandlot is on the edge of town, Senseney's Woods. Beyond it marks the end of civilization as Spottswood knows it. For a place no respectable person is supposed to know about, a great many find their way here.

A group of African American youths, all larger than Spottswood, are in the final stages of setting up a baseball game as he arrives. Everyone wears ragged clothing, making Spottswood's fine apparel more conspicuous. The field is rocky with old flour sacks serving as bases.

The older players on the opposing team laugh as Spottswood joins his teammates.

"Run out of men?" they tease. "Is that the best you can do? Give us our money now, country boys."

One of Spottswood's teammates, Sam Crawford, takes him to one side. "Do your usual."

Spottswood, a left-handed batter, heads toward the plate as the game begins (the other team has claimed "last licks," not really believing they will need them). The players on the other team laugh and catcall. Their pitcher motions them to move in. Spottswood digs in, his body tense, his face an angry mask. Once he assumes his batting stance, not a muscle in his body moves, save for his fingers, which play in nervous anticipation along the bat's handle.

At first taken aback by Spottswood's intensity, the pitcher, a stout young man of about twenty, taunts the batter. "If you scrunch your face like that you're gonna pee yourself."

Laughter and more taunting come from the field.

"Never mind him, Spotts." Sam's voice is reassuring.

"Spot this, little pecker."

The pitcher rears back and unleashes a fastball down the middle of the plate. With a compact swing, Spottswood whistles a liner past the pitcher's ear, sending the pitcher to the ground in fear and the ball into center field. The bat resonates from its heart as Spottswood hits the ball, having caught the best part of the sweet spot. It is a sound apart from the normal crack of the bat. The pitcher sits helplessly on his rump, flapping his arms, screaming at his fielders to get the ball as it disappears into the depths of the outfield (grass grows tall in this area, and the occasional snake is a home-field advantage).

Spottswood, running incredibly fast, rounds second before an outfielder can touch the ball. He's at third before the relay man gets his throw and halfway to the plate by the time the ball heads home.

Spottswood rams full force into the catcher before the ball, which comes in high, can reaches its target. The catcher gets up as if to fight, but Spottswood descends on him as quickly as he runs, fists flying, with most of the blows finding their mark. Spottswood's teammates pull him off the dazed catcher, who takes several moments to shake off the effects of Spottswood's attack before murmuring a string of obscenities.

A few of a growing number of spectators pass money between them; a few push money into Spottswood's pockets as he passes by them on the way to the fallen tree that serves as his team's bench.

The game goes on as games usually do when Spottswood plays. He hits everything thrown at him and catches everything that is hit his way or slightly beyond it in the outfield. Spottswood plays a shallow center field, catching balls that would usually fall in for singles. His speed allows him to do this; breaking back at the crack of the bat and pulling in long drives over his shoulder. His glove is burlap cushioned with a bit of straw. Spottswood learns how to anticipate a ball so that it doesn't smack the meat of his hand. Still, between baseball and never-ending chores, his hands are tough and calloused by the time he is ten.

The field's inconsistencies lead to wild caroms and the worst of bad hops. Spottswood studies these inconsistencies until each is an ally. He anticipates bad hops, faking runners into trying to take an extra base and easily throwing them out.

The game is going well until Lucy bursts forth from behind the crowd. Although small, she carries with her a force of purpose that compels men to get out of her way. She grabs Spottswood by the collar as he is about to bat, and the other youths run in a hundred different directions. Lucy takes Spottswood, his feet barely touching the ground, through the crowd.

Spottswood hears his mother cursing under her breath (what else could she being saying?) as they make their way back to civilization and the house on Water Street.

The door of the large house slams shut behind them, and Lucy half throws Spottswood into Major Conrad's study. The room's two desks are piled high with papers. Books clog the shelves lining the wall, some stacked at angles and atop one another. A small fire, almost like an eternal flame, burns in the fireplace no matter how hot the weather. Into these flames, Major Conrad consigns papers that are no longer of use or those he considers unfit for public view or preservation.

A lot of Winchester's secrets die in the office's fireplace.

Major Conrad is working intently. He moves papers from one large pile on his desk to another as he talks to himself under his breath. He is annoyed when Spottswood, with Lucy close behind, is thrust into his sanctuary. He begins bellowing without looking up.

"Never disturb a man at his business!"

"I will disturb you at your business because I have disturbed the devil at his!"

Major Conrad puts down the papers, removes his glasses, and rubs his hand several times over his face in a weary motion. "What has he done?"

"Played baseball when he should have been at revival!"

"Baseball. Another Yankee imposition on our culture. I remember—"

"Enough about the Yankees! We're talking about this child's soul."

"I thought we were talking about baseball."

"The kind of people who hang about those games!"

Major Conrad reaches out and places his hand on Spottswood's shoulder. "Did you win?"

"We did! And I hit—"

Spottswood's sentence is interrupted by his mother's slap to the side of his head. She glares at Major Conrad.

"Did he win? I'll show you what he won!"

Lucy takes the small wad of bills she seized from Spottswood and throws it in front of Major Conrad. Major Conrad is motionless for a moment as he regards the money. "This is a very different matter. Could you please excuse us, Lucy."

Lucy storms from the room.

"Did he win! The stupidity men fall to over hitting a ball!"

Major Conrad places the boy directly in front of him. The older man moves his face close to the boy's and speaks with added gravity. "Playing for the love of sport is one thing. I believe the Lord could forgive you that. Playing for money on the Sabbath—your mother is right about the kind of people who are about baseball games. You are above them."

"But the others take money. The others—"

"—do not live under my roof."

Major Conrad takes the money and places it in the fireplace. The bills curl as they burn and are soon reduced to ashes.

Tom has been watching this scene from a corner. He approaches his father as Spottswood leaves the room. Tom looks at the fire.

"Can we afford to be burning money?"

"If it's badly earned."

"We can't afford servants. We should keep what they bring in."

"I will decide what we can and can't afford."

"You could put them out. They'd find a way to live."

A look of anger passes across Major Conrad's face. "Our family has provided their home for four generations—slave and free. If they leave, it will be of their own accord, not by my order."

"But—"

Major Conrad holds up his hand. "This discussion has reached its conclusion."

Sunday dinner is eaten in silence, four people around a large table lost in their own thoughts. Spottswood confines his field of vision to his plate. He feels his mother's eyes burning into him.

As the afternoon turns to dusk, Lucy is washing dishes in the kitchen when she hears a series of dull, un-rhythmic thumps coming from the backyard. Looking across the room she sees an axe leaning against an empty wood box. Grabbing the axe, she storms out the door.

On the back porch, she stops when she sees Major Conrad watching something intently. He extends his arm to halt Lucy.

In the backyard, Spottswood has tied a ball of rags to a tall tree limb with a long strand of rope. When he strikes the makeshift ball with his bat, it stretches the rope to its limit, then comes back at varying angles. No sooner has he hit the ball than Spottswood quickly resumes his batting stance and tenses for its next assault.

He hits the ball every time.

"Anyone can chop wood." With those words, Major Conrad turns and leads Lucy into the house, leaving Spottswood at his business.

Chapter Three

A LIFE OF SERVICE

SPOTTSWOOD DEDICATES HIS YOUNG LIFE to becoming an indispensable servant.

A formal education is not part of his training.

Major Conrad asks Lucy when she will send Spottswood to school, which is not required for people of color. Her answer is always the same: "All the education he needs, I can give him. Books will only put before him that which can't be had by people like us. It will lead to a life of longing and discontent or, worse, create an angry man who will be a danger to himself and everyone near him."

She often punctuates these observations with the story about the African American man who was dragged from the train in Stephens City and lynched. "He was going to a place he didn't belong in too grand a style. Spottswood will not die at the end of a rope."

What time he spends away from the house on Water Street, Spottswood plays baseball or works on the ancestral Conrad farm off Valley Pike on the outskirts of town. The road to the farm is paved—paid for by an ambitious turnpike master who charged the Federals a penny apiece on their advances and retreats through the

Shenandoah Valley. An avowed Confederate, the turnpike master is as amazed as any when the government, several years after the war, pays him based on notches carved in hundreds of sticks.

Reminders of the war are all along the Valley Pike.

Each spring, plows unearth unfortunate souls left behind in the heat of battle. Work stops, and no matter which side the bones' allegiance betrays, a minister is called, words spoken, and a proper burial conducted among the anonymous Federal and Confederate dead.

Bones are not the most unnerving thing the plows unearth.

Unexploded shells are struck at alarmingly frequent intervals. The black powder inside has grown unstable with age and the shells are handled carefully, if at all, before being detonated as safely as possible.

More benign reminders are the bullets often found in rows, marking long-ago skirmish lines. Major Conrad explains to Spottswood that these rounds are "drops," bullets sent to the ground by fumbling fingers in the heat of combat or dropped when their unfortunate owner is struck. The soft lead in bullets used during the war makes them flatten on impact, causing horrible exit wounds, shattered bones, and lingering deaths for those not fortunate enough to be killed outright. A perfectly intact bullet is a bullet that was never fired.

One warm October afternoon, Spottswood sees a stranger in a back meadow of the Conrad farm sitting beneath a tree. He wears a traveler's suit with a wide-brimmed hat that obscures his features. Spottswood summons Major Conrad from the barn and wonders if he should ask the man his business on private property.

"He fought here. Leave him in peace. He may stay as long as he wishes."

"He was in the army with you?"

"No. He was a Federal."

"Why is he welcome to stay?"

Major Conrad leans against a fence and watches the man intently as he speaks.

"His name is Major Joseph Stearns, late of the 1st New York Cavalry. When Sheridan took the Valley, he ordered all crops and livestock destroyed so the Confederacy would starve. Custer and his Michigan Wolverines took delight in such work. They would set barns afire at dusk and proceed up the Valley, methodically burning one after another. All the poor farmers could do was watch in the darkness, knowing they would be the next to fall under the torch. It was savage what they did to Custer in the Montana Territory. There are those who say he deserved it.

"Major Stearns was tasked with burning Stephens City to the ground in June of '64. Looking about, he saw only the old and sick, women, children; he refused to put it to the torch and said he'd shoot any man who did. Such humanity is rare in war. It is not every man who'll refuse to strike a blow on a helpless enemy. It is a sign of goodness that transcends circumstance. Major Stearns is a good man. It is my honor to have him sit in my meadow as long as he likes."

After a long silence, Spottswood picks up his end of the conversation.

"What is he looking for?"

"His youth. His humanity. Friends long gone. I look for them myself in these fields."

"Did you fight here?"

"First and Second Kernstown, early in the war. Stonewall Jackson was our commander. Won the first battle, fought to a draw in the second on a Sunday; Jackson said fighting on the Lord's Day unnerved him. I never comprehended how a man so indifferent to slaughter—the enemy and his own troops—would be unnerved by fighting on the Sabbath, as if any other day were fine for such godless work."

Major Stearns is not the only former Federal seeking to reconcile his past in Winchester and its environs.

Rudolph Whistler is a fifteen-year-old private from New Hampshire when he first comes to Winchester in the winter of 1864–65. Having no hope of seeing the front because of his age, Rudolph is stationed outside Conrad House to protect its esteemed occupant, former Delegate George Washington Conrad.

The Federals' attitude toward this pillar of Winchester society varies during the war. At its outset, he is taken prisoner and sent to Fort McHenry in Baltimore. The prevailing wisdom at the time is that holding prominent citizens hostage will ensure good behavior in border areas. That having failed, George Washington Conrad is returned to Winchester in the fall of 1862 and placed under guard when the Federals are in control of the town.

The Conrad patriarch's first take on seeing young Whistler standing sentry at his doorway is "You are guarding me, but who is guarding you?" A familiarity grows between them in the coming months and continues through the years as Whistler becomes a Presbyterian minister. He will sometimes co-preside over reconciliation services that are held with increasing frequency as the nineteenth century edges toward the twentieth.

Members of the Grand Army of the Republic sometimes arrive en masse to dedicate a battlefield monument or decorate the graves of fallen comrades. Directing them to the sites of their former heroism proves vexing for the locals, as they did not agree with their conquerors as to how things should be referred to.

Star Fort, which guards the western side of the town, is the name used by the Federals. To the locals, it is known as Fort Alabama, its Confederate name. Federals name their battles after the nearest body of water, Confederates the nearest town. Thus, the "Battle of the Opequon" and the "Battle of Winchester" refer to the same event.

It is almost as if the two sides perpetuate the divisions of the Civil War as though nothing has been decided.

This conflict in finding a common vocabulary mirrors the feelings Spottswood develops for the Civil War. On the one hand, his freedom is won by the Federals. On the other, he cannot imagine how someone as noble as Major Conrad would devote himself to an ignoble cause.

Next to the ball field, the farm is the place Spottswood feels most at home. He especially likes learning how to maintain the farm machinery; mechanics comes easily to him. Spottswood instinctively sees how various gears and levers work together to create a synchronous whole.

Lucy tolerates the farm but sees Spottswood's future as a house servant, a gentleman's gentleman. She frets every time the sweaty, dirty, and happy child bounds into the kitchen.

"I will not raise a field hand."

Lucy is always busy.

That is the price of being meticulous and paying attention to every detail, no matter how minor. She teaches Spottswood the finer points of a fine life that might have once existed within the walls of the house on Water Street.

Formal dining is central to this life. Lucy instructs Spottswood in the etiquette behind maintaining a formal dinner setting so as not to expose the host to the whispered daggers of social ridicule.

"The first thing that must go on the table is the baize." With this

Lucy places a thick, burgundy cloth over the battered top of the oaken table, which has been extended from its domestic size to a grander expanse through the addition of mismatched leaves. "Linen is thin. With a splash of color beneath it, it appears a fine accent. Left alone, it reveals the flaws in the table beneath its transparency."

Lucy's language always elevates to the task, fine words for a grand labor.

After placing the linen, she places small silver bouquet holders, long and thin, at each lady's setting. Smaller squat silver bowls denote the place where gentlemen will sit.

"In summer, cut roses from the garden about an hour before the dinner and place eight in the bouquet holders and four—it's called a boutonnière—before the gentleman's place."

"Why don't men get bouquets?"

"Because, like few things in this life, they are reserved for the pleasure of women."

During one of these sessions, which Spottswood finds less than absorbing, he thinks to ask his mother a question that such quiet moments may allow.

"Who is my father?"

The silverware that Lucy is placing on the table falls from her grasp with a clatter followed by prolonged silence as she gathers her thoughts.

"Your father is an honorable man."

"Can I see him?"

"He watches over you and makes sure you are protected from the cruelties of life."

"What does he do?"

"He does enough to provide for us. He provides for us and watches out for us."

"What—"

"That is all you need know."

"But . . ."

Lucy begins arranging the silverware next to each place setting.

"Knives and spoons on the right side, forks on the left. Arrange them from the outside in: appetizer, salad, entrée, dessert. If you place them in the proper order, your guest won't be confused. Everything has a proper place."

"But . . ."

"Everything has a proper place. If life ran like a dinner table, everyone would know their role and be happy. Things would go as planned."

Lucy folds a napkin upon the plate. Beneath its top fold, she places a small piece of bread, an inch thick and three inches long.

"This is what is called an expected surprise. People expect to find a piece of bread or such in the folds of the napkin. They expect it but are always surprised—and gratified—to find it."

Next, Lucy brings carafes to the table.

"Fill these with cool water that you've kept in the ice box, but only for an hour, no more. These are just big enough to hold two glasses of water for each guest. Only a horse would drink more."

Spottswood laughs. Having broken the tension, at least where he is concerned, Spottswood resumes his line of questioning.

"Who is—"

Lucy stops again, this time the flush of her face betraying more than a little anger.

"What have I been teaching you?"

"How to set—"

Lucy throws up her arms in exasperation.

"Order and place! It is not your place to ask such questions."

"Why is this my place?"

"God has a plan for us all, and his plan placed you here with me in this lovely home with someone who watches over us."

"Will I always live here?"

"God will let you know when his plan changes. That's what happened when he had Moses lead the Israelites out of Egypt. Change is hard. Don't pray for change. Be happy for what you have. It's more than most people have."

Composing herself for a moment, Lucy picks up a stack of plates. "Plates for each course should be kept, stacked in the order of use, on the sideboard."

THE LAVENDER ROOM

Chapter Four

OF ALL THE RULES that abound in the large yellow house on Water Street, one stands above all others: no one is to enter the room at the end of the second floor hall except for Lucy, who cleans it once a week. The room is a monument to the absent lady of the house and represents a hope that its maintenance will lead to her return.

Adelaide Hanratty is the cousin of Judge John Handley, a man considered both a savior and a devil, sometimes in the same sentence, by the people of Winchester. Born in Ireland and raised in Pennsylvania from a young age, Judge Handley made a fortune during the war selling anthracite coal to the Federals to fuel the endless stream of trains heading south. He did the minimum four months of service in the Union army before returning to the one thing he does best in life: making money.

To ensure his business is unmolested, he procures a law degree and, shortly thereafter, a magistrate's position. Although his judicial domain includes petty business disputes and land matters, Handley wears the title of "judge" like a Supreme Court jurist's robes. A fine mustache and flowing hair give him the aura of judicial majesty.

The folk of Scranton, Pennsylvania, where the Judge makes his fortune, are none too enamored of his lack of service or willingness to make a dollar off the great cause of his generation. He finds more amiable company in Winchester (the rebellious nature of the Confederacy speaks to something within his Irish soul). He finds a particularly kindred spirit in Dr. Hunter Maguire.

Before the war, Doctor Maguire established and ran the Winchester Medical College at the corner of Stewart and Boscawen streets. Buoyed by the prospect of applying their knowledge to the violently injured, several students took the journey to Harper's Ferry at the height of John Brown's raid. Outside of town, they found the body of a man later identified as Watson Brown, the would-be messiah's son. Delighted that they would not have to raid local cemeteries for a cadaver on which to practice their art, the medical students haul Watson back to Winchester in the general confusion that follows the first act of the coming war.

When General Nathaniel Banks and the Federals first occupied Winchester, they found Watson's skeleton in a closet with a placard reading "Old John Brown" around its neck. Stoked with abolitionist fury, they removed Watson for a proper burial and put the college to the torch. Ironically, the first man killed in the Brown Raid was Heywood Shepherd, a free African American who lived on Winchester's Kent Street. He was working as a baggage master for the Winchester & Potomac Railroad in Harper's Ferry when he saw Brown's men approaching the federal arsenal and began to run. Not wishing to be detected, Brown's men shot a free African American dead so that they could incite a revolt to free slaves. Of course, the shot woke the townspeople and ultimately led to the raid's failure. Shepherd's fate illustrates the complexities that face generations of African Americans in Winchester and its neighboring towns.

His academic career ended by his student's collection of a historic cadaver, Doctor Maguire enlisted in the Confederate army. His most famous patient was Stonewall Jackson, a dear friend after Jackson's prolonged stay in Winchester after Banks was driven from the town. Despite their friendship, Maguire effectively killed Jackson by amputating his left arm after a devastating friendly fire incident at Chancellorsville.

In unguarded moments, Major Conrad wonders how a man who has brought such disaster upon those around him can enjoy the fine reputation of Doctor Maguire. (His puzzlement only grows as Maguire is eventually appointed surgeon general of the United States.)

Judge Handley's first attempt at restoring Winchester's fortunes was a resort based on the sulfur springs found throughout the town. Major Conrad also ruminates, again in unguarded moments, why people will pay to sit in water they won't drink. (His sentiments are shared by the tourists, who stay away from the sulfur-spring bathhouses in droves.) Another amenity imported from Pennsylvania, golf, isn't enough to save the resort, and a good deal of Winchester's citizens lose their life savings in the aftermath.

Then, in 1895, Judge Handley performs the greatest service he can for the beleaguered citizens of Winchester.

He dies.

He dies, but not before being angered by the citizens of Scranton. Tired of his courting Southerners and of the dubious origins of his fortune, the people of Scranton erect a pig pen before the Judge's house on the market square. To that point, the Judge, a divorcé whose only son died in childhood, has left 50 percent of his wealth to Winchester and 50 percent to Scranton in his will. Now amended, the will bestows on Winchester the whole fortune, the vast sum of 1.2 million dollars. In years to come, the money builds the Handley Library, Handley High School, and the Douglass School. (Well into the twenty-first century, the schoolchildren of Winchester march to Judge Handley's tomb in Stonewall Cemetery to heap bouquets and equally flowery words upon their benefactor.)

All of that is years in the future when Holmes Conrad first lays eyes on Adelaide Hanratty at the Mason's Harvest Ball in 1878.

They made a striking couple; none could deny it.

The courtly Major Conrad, by now forty, was a local source of fascination. Distinguished and handsome, he was sought by every eligible woman—and some women who wished they were eligible—in Winchester and the surrounding counties.

Nobody seemed to catch is eye and keep it until Adelaide. Pleasingly plump by the standards of her day, her most striking feature was her violet eyes, which provided a beautiful contrast to the raven hair that cascaded to her shoulders. Only twenty-one, she captured the Major with her quick wit as much as her physical attractiveness.

They married in 1880. Tom arrived in 1882.

But depression soon engulfed her.

Major Conrad's role as state senator means he must spend every January through March in Richmond. The funereal atmosphere of the "Holy City on the James," coupled with the gray of winter, left Adelaide virtually unable to move from her hotel room on Broad Street. A pall of a different type, social ostracism of Major Conrad's "Yankee folly," left her more isolated. The grand dames of Richmond, all bearing the title "Mrs." before names like Lee, Jackson, and Stewart, did not include Adelaide as they laid plans to sanitize and monumentalize the "Lost Cause."

Major Conrad did not realize the depths of his wife's depression until their own cause was lost.

May 31, 1889 proved a bit of hope for Adelaide, though she didn't really perceive it at the time. On that date, Pennsylvania's South Fork Dam broke, condemning 2,200 unfortunate souls down the valley to a horrible death in what became known as "the Johnstown Flood."

Maintained by a group of wealthy residents of Pittsburgh— Andrew Carnegie chief among them—under the name of the South Fork Hunting and Fishing Club, the dam had been considered structurally unsound for years.

Soon, everyone associated with the club (not named Carnegie), was looking for an area to relocate. Judge Handley's toehold established, many opted for Winchester. A fine mansion, dedicated to the Baker family of chocolate fame, soon rose at the corner of Washington and Boscawen streets. Other fine homes, in the Victorian and Federal styles, soon joined it. The locals groused about "a second Yankee invasion," but not so loudly as to stop the flow of much-needed cash into their community.

For a time, Adelaide found solace among these refugees with Dutch and German names. She also gained introduction to those in the upper strata of society with whom they were acquainted. By 1893, Adelaide was taking winter sojourns to New York, leaving Major Conrad and Tom in Lucy's care, and summering in Newport among the Vanderbilts and Whitneys.

By 1897, she was gone altogether.

A prominent Pittsburgh family, the Thaws, allotted her a small suite in a second-tier New York hotel for the social season, and there was always room in Newport's finer homes during the summer.

By the turn of the century, all that was left of Adelaide in Winchester was the second-floor shrine in the house on Water Street.

The door was unlocked.

Spottswood finds himself standing in the one room into which he is not allowed. Natural curiosity overcomes his mother's stern dictates.

The room is done all in lavender; full, flowing curtains; a four-poster bed with a fine quilt; white dresser and chair, gilded at their edges; and a full-length mirror. A lavender dress is draped over a dress maker's form at one side of the bed, making it appear at a glance to be worn by a ghost. A wash basin and series of brushes and combs are laid out as though they will soon be used.

One wall is dominated by a large wedding photograph of Major Conrad and Adelaide. She beams happily above a massive white dress and beneath an elaborate tiara. Major Conrad looks stiff and reserved in his black wedding suit. What strikes Spottswood is his mentor's relative youth. Spottswood never thinks of Major Conrad as a young man.

In the hallway, Lucy lets out a small shriek, as much to acknowledge her own carelessness as what she sees before her. Before the sound can completely leave her lips, a figure steps into the doorway between her and Spottswood.

Tom steps behind Spottswood and gently grasps his shoulders, causing only mild alarm in the boy. Tom turns Spottswood and guides him slowly from the room, allowing Spottswood one last moment to turn and look over his shoulder.

Spottswood is taken outside the room and left standing before his mother in the hallway.

Tom closes the door and locks it.

He places the key in his pocket and walks down the hallway, down the stairs, and out the front door.

Tom is always standoffish where Spottswood is concerned, with one notable exception.

A cool fall evening finds Spottswood, now in his early teens, coming down Valley Avenue from the farm. The last orange light of day is fading when Spottswood finds himself near the old Episcopal Church on Boscawen Street. In a courtyard next to the church is the aboveground tomb of Thomas, Lord Fairfax, George Washington's benefactor and the original holder of the land now occupied by Winchester. Spottswood is well aware of the legendary sightings of the ghost of the English nobleman, whom locals say is still bitter about his lands being confiscated by his former subjects.

Overwhelmed by fear, Spottswood doesn't hear footsteps coming behind him. The first time there is an indication that he is in any danger is when a solid blow lands on the right side of his head, knocking him to his knees. Stunned, Spottswood collapses to the ground as more blows, each more vicious than the last, rain upon him.

Looking up from his back after what seems like an eternity, Spottswood sees himself surrounded by gray uniforms that mark those who wear them as students at the nearby Shenandoah Academy. One youth, Marshall, appears to be the ringleader. He is a tall, wiry youth, whose most prominent features are burning blue eyes and a shock of blonde hair that shoots like a geyser from his forehead. Spottswood notices his own blood dripping from one of Marshall's knuckles as he stares upward in a dazed state.

"Looks like we caught us a little house nigger walking through a white neighborhood." The words drip from Marshall's mouth and fall upon Spottswood with the force of spit. "You lookin' in windows, boy? What makes you think you have the right to be here?"

There is laughter mixed with malicious words from those encircling Spottswood. "I asked you a question," the words leap in a shout from Marshall's mouth. He is about to deliver another blow when his nose appears to explode.

After a moment of numbed disbelief, Spottswood looks up to see Tom hitting Marshall with a succession of increasingly violent blows. Those who try to intercede are knocked backward by Tom's fury, until none are left to defend Marshall, whose semi-conscious form, blood pouring from several head wounds, is soon lying next to Spottswood's.

"Get him out of here. Get him out of here!" Spottswood has never heard rage in Tom's voice before. After a tense moment, the others scoop Marshall off the pavement and disappear into the growing darkness.

Tom is a frustrated man of action.

His contemporaries, especially the Byrd brothers, seem to have eclipsed him with an early life of exceptional achievement.

Richard Byrd, once the speaker of the Virginia House of Delegates, lives near the railroad tracks on Amherst Street. His sons harbor a burning desire to succeed that seems the polar opposite of their father's mild amiability.

The oldest, Harry, takes over the family's failing newspaper, *The Winchester Evening Star*, at fifteen. Each morning, he boards a train next to his home for a trip to Martinsburg, West Virginia, to buy newsprint. Harry develops a "pay-as-you-go" philosophy that eventually leads to the governor's mansion and the Senate.

Harry's brother, Richard, known as "Dick," is an impossibly handsome, athletic youth whose lust for adventure exceeds his parents' control. When he was twelve, they let Dick travel to the Philippines to fight pirates. This daring spirit eventually leads to a life of polar exploration.

Tom feels decidedly inferior to such contemporaries. His father refuses to sign an age waiver that would allow Tom to enlist to fight the Spanish. (Eventually, after many heated discussions, Tom joins the National Guard.) Tom feels, though, that his life will never be heroic. At this moment, as Tom helps Spottswood to his feet, there is no greater hero in Spottswood's eyes than Tom Conrad.

Whether the result of delayed fear, anger, or shame, Spottswood finds himself doing something he rarely does—crying. The tears burn and sting as they pour down his cheeks. Tom dries Spottswood's tears and hands him his handkerchief, which Spottswood fumbles with before Tom guides it into Spottswood's pocket.

Tom takes Spottswood's hand, and they begin walking home.

"You're a hero." The words come softly out of Spottswood's mouth.

Tom shakes his head no. "I am a replacement."

"For who?"

"*Whom*. My Uncle Thomas."

"I've never heard of him."

"It is a very painful subject where father is concerned. Thomas was his younger brother by two years. When the War Between the States began, it was decided they would join separate units to lessen the chance that they would both be lost in battle."

"But Thomas was lost?"

"Guarding the Rappahannock Bridge. Federal raiding party, a very minor action. A courier rode through the night to inform Grandfather, who went to Rappahannock immediately despite the number of Federals roaming the area. He found Thomas near the bridge. Someone had taken his boots and sword. Father says he would kill the man who took them if he could be identified. Grandfather was told it was too dangerous to bring Thomas back to Winchester, so he persuaded a local farmer to bury him in the family plot.

"The war was hard-fought in that area. The farm was burned, the farmer driven from his land, and all traces of the cemetery obliterated. Grandfather and Father went back to the area for years but could never find Thomas. That is a pain that nags at Father still."

As Tom and Spottswood reach the gaslights that mark the edge of Winchester's business district, Tom releases Spottswood's hand and walks ahead.

OUT-OF-TOWN VISITOR

IN THE SPRING OF 1907, Spottswood, not yet twenty, is the dominant center fielder in the Shenandoah Valley. The local African American teams that he plays on—there are several—range as far as southern Pennsylvania, Baltimore, and Washington. Whenever a team faces a big game, a representative is dispatched to the kitchen door of the house on Water Street seeking Spottswood. Lucy always tries to shoo such messengers away, but Spottswood is past her and out the door before her protests reach their conclusion. He keeps a bag of equipment always at the ready. Spottswood's fame grows, though he pretends not to notice.

Tom is the only member of the household who openly helps Spottswood in his passion. When he notices the discomfort Spottswood's first pair of baseball spikes cause him, Thomas takes the shoes to the harness shop on Fairfax Lane and has them stretched until they are a perfect fit. Tom also commissions the harness maker to sew Spottswood a proper fielder's mitt based on an illustration in the Police Gazette.

Spottswood pretends not to notice the young women who hang

around the bench before and after games seeking his attention. While Spottswood has feelings toward young women, he doesn't want emotion to override common sense or disrupt his future, which he sees lying beyond the confines of the comfortable life of his upbringing.

On a particular day, uneventful at its beginning, a baseball sails high through a cloudless blue sky.

"Spotts, your ball!" Crawford calls from left field.

"Always is."

The ball lands surely in a glove at the end of an outstretched arm. Spottswood is a muscular, compact young man. An ill-fitting, hand-me-down uniform can't hide a sculpted body. A large crowd, applauding, watches as he runs back to the dugout. Spottswood has gotten used to this and briefly tips his cap. As he runs past Crawford, Spottswood pats Crawford's ample stomach disapprovingly, something a much-older veteran player would do.

One person is not applauding.

Hiram Laycock, known in scouting circles as "Fishpaw," looks down at a small leather notebook, recording notes in a slow, steady hand. He licks his pencil at intervals, as much to gather his thoughts as anything. A large, African American man, Fishpaw sweats in a full suit, topped by a newly blocked bowler. He is clearly not used to southern humidity.

Before Spottswood reaches the bench, Sam grabs his shoulder and guides him to where Fishpaw is standing.

"Is he everything I said?"

"At this level," Fishpaw barely acknowledges Sam as he scrawls in his notebook.

Fishpaw reaches into his pocket and produces a wad of money. He peels off a five and hands it to Sam. He waves Sam away in the manner of royalty dismissing a servant before turning to Spottswood.

"Let us talk."

Spottswood turns away but is held by Fishpaw's massive hand on his shoulder. He shoots Fishpaw a glance bordering on anger.

"I don't associate with gamblers."

"Neither do I, unless I have a sure thing."

"I have a game to play."

"Not here."

"Who are you?"

"Name's Fishpaw. I have a longer one, but that's the one I use when I'm doing business. I'm a scout for Mr. Abe Rothstein, owner of the New York Elite Giants."

"You're crazy."

"To be in this godforsaken place when I could be strolling down Broadway, you may have a point."

"I don't know any New York Elite Giants, or any Abe . . ."

". . . Rothstein. The New York Elite Giants are the premiere Negro team in America. Our manager is Moses Walker, used to play for Toledo in the American Association."

"I've never heard of a Negro professional team."

"And you're not likely to, here."

Spottswood thinks a moment before responding. "You will have to ask my family."

"I don't want to marry you."

"Dinner at seven. The large yellow house on Water Street across from city hall."

Spottswood goes back to the bench as Fishpaw lets out an exasperated sigh. "You had better be worth the effort."

That evening's meal is eventful and unusual on many fronts.

Spottswood watches as Major Conrad sits at the head of a large table, perfectly set; Lucy and Spottswood on one side, Fishpaw on the other, and Tom at the other end. At the center, as always, is a large lazy Susan covered with condiments and side dishes. It makes a rumbling noise when spun.

"I understand you wish Spottswood to play baseball profession-ally," Major Conrad's tone is incredulous.

"You understand correctly," says Fishpaw maintaining eye contact while simultaneously cutting his roast beef (Spottswood is amazed by the dexterity involved).

"This would be in New York?"

"Correct. That is our home base, but we play at all points east of the Mississippi and north of Washington."

Major Conrad turns the lazy Susan so that toast is in front of Fishpaw.

"Toast?"

"An unusual choice for supper."

"When I served in the War Between the States, many was the day—or night—when I was grateful for toast. Burning the bread brings out the flavor of the grain."

Fishpaw takes a piece of toast.

"Indeed. I notice by the state of the houses in Winchester—and this is just an observation—that there must have been a great deal of fighting here."

"Winchester changed hands seventy-two times during the war, which I believe is a record. Mr. Potts on Jefferson Street kept count. I don't know why, considering the danger involved."

"Seventy-two times! I pray I do not have to be as persistent."

"Persistence is a characteristic of dubious virtue." Lucy doesn't look up from her plate as the words spill out.

"Too true. I shall stay to the point, Missus—I'm sorry, is it Missus or Miss Poles?"

"It's Lucy."

Lucy turns the lazy Susan so that honey is in front of Fishpaw.

"Honey. It adds sweetness."

Fishpaw spreads honey on the toast. "I must say—and this is just an observation—that I have never seen whites and coloreds eat at the same table beneath the Pennsylvania line, not even in the more enlightened parts of Maryland."

This observation diverts Tom's attention from his roast beef. "My father considers our household staff as members of the family. He is sentimental."

Lucy turns the lazy Susan so that a bowl of pickles is in front of Fishpaw. "Pickle? I made them myself."

Major Conrad feels compelled to explain the situation.

"Tom, Lucy, and Spottswood were born in this house. We are as family."

Fishpaw spins the lazy Susan with a bit too much force. The food upon it almost falls off, but not quite. It comes to rest with some of its elements out of place.

"To the point: Lucy, would you sign a contract allowing Spottswood to join the New York Elite Giants?"

"I cannot."

"You won't?"

"I cannot read or write. I am a lady of the house. There is no need."

Major Conrad breaks the silence that follows.

"Should Lucy assent, she can make her mark, and I will sign her name and attest to the veracity of the transaction."

That said, dinner continues at a social, genial pace.

Such is not the case an hour later in Major Conrad's office. Lucy sits weeping in the corner. Spottswood stands before Major Conrad, who fumbles absently with his papers as he tries to deal with the situation before him.

"He will die among demons in New York. It is hell on earth!"

Major Conrad turns toward Lucy with a reassuring glance. "I have been there on business. It is not hell, just a suburb."

"He barely knows how to read."

"Something I tried to remedy."

"Reading will only show him things he can't have. He belongs here."

"Just because you are born in a place does not mean you belong there."

"He has a place here, knows his family."

"She's right in one regard, Spottswood: you have no one in New York."

"I know enough to stay away from the wrong kind. You taught me that."

"The right kind can be even more dangerous."

"How is that?"

Major Conrad goes to the mantel, over which hangs an officer's sword in its scabbard. He takes the sword from its place of honor and absently pulls back on its handle, exposing a small part of the blade.

"When I was not that much older than you, twenty-three to be exact, I took my father's place in the House of Delegates in Richmond. He could not bring himself to make the choice between Virginia and the United States, so I was selected to vote on behalf of our community. I was awed to be there. President Tyler sat two chairs from me. Twice I stood and voted against secession. All those around me, all the right people, they had passionate arguments about states' rights and the sovereignty of Virginia. At length, they carried the day."

"Why didn't you come home? Why did you fight for something you didn't believe was right?" Spottswood has never before asked this question.

"When you're young, you are at times swept away by the magnitude of events around you. I did not believe in slavery. I did believe in defending my home. The larger issue was obscured by the more immediate. I did not lay down my arms until Appomattox. I have not taken them up since."

Major Conrad firmly shoves the blade into the scabbard and replaces the sword above the mantel.

"You know how I feel. I have to go." Spottswood's observation is a statement, not a plea.

Major Conrad takes the contract and lays it upon his desk for Lucy to sign. Hands trembling, she makes a quick *X* and turns away. Major Conrad considers the contract for a moment then signs in a long, measured hand. He takes a lawyer's official stamp, rolls it in ink, and stamps a seal next to his signature.

"That is so much quicker and neater than the wax seal my father used."

"There is nothing quick or neat about this." Spottswood cannot tell if his mother is trembling with fear or rage as she looks down on the contract.

Major Conrad grasps Spottswood by the shoulders.

"Never disgrace us. Never sell that which you love for momentary gain. Earn your money. Earn it fairly. Never drink or gamble. If you maintain your dignity, all else of worth will follow."

"Yes, sir."

The next morning finds Spottswood, dressed in an ill-fitting suit once owned by Tom, running for a train, at the same time trying to contain the clothes that bulge from his suitcase. Major Conrad watches his hurried departure; Lucy declined to come. Fishpaw, standing on a platform at the rear of the train, pulls a gold watch from his pocket, gives an exasperated sigh, and replaces it.

"I hope to God New York is more ready for you than you are for it."

MOSES

Chapter Six

AFTER SETTLING INTO A CHEAP BOARDING HOUSE that Fishpaw recommends, Spottswood makes his way to the Polo Grounds, the Elite Giants' home stadium. (Fishpaw's recommendation is based as much upon philosophy as economy. He says if Spottswood's accommodations are too grand, he will not wish to leave them and explore all New York has to offer.) Keeping in mind the serious business before him allows Spottswood to block out the sheer size of New York and the commotion that swirls about him at dizzying speed as he heads to the city's premiere stadium.

As a final part of his scouting duties, Fishpaw acts as guide, moving Spottswood through the subway and down the Grand Concourse that leads to the Polo Grounds. Spottswood is amazed by the sheer size of the stadium—sixteen thousand seats. However, he spies something familiar at its perimeter: spectators in horse-drawn buggies watch the action just beyond a board-and-wire fence that marks the end of the playing field.

Despite doing everything at double time with Fishpaw bellowing instructions at any gap in movement, Spottswood arrives at the stadium after the game has begun. An indifferent equipment man gives him an ill-fitting uniform that screams "rube" and "bush-leaguer." (Numbers are still an innovation some years into the future. Eventually, Spottswood wears number 23. Decades later when Willie Mays wears number 24 while roaming the Polo Grounds' vast center field, Spottswood jokes that Mays chose the number because he was following Spottswood.) Spottswood tucks and gathers as best he can to make the uniform look professional.

He fails.

The New York Elite Giants play before a small, enthusiastic crowd. The dugout is the domain of manager Moses Fleetwood Walker, a muscular ex-catcher. Walker's body has rounded a bit into middle age with the exception of his eyes, which shoot daggers. He looks at the field with disdain, a look that turns to disgust when he sees Spottswood sneaking onto a corner of the bench.

"Who dare comes into my dugout without so much as an introduction?" All eyes turn toward Spottswood.

Spottswood looks aimlessly about for a moment.

"I mean you, Hayseed!"

"My name's Spottswood."

"Spottswood Poles from Virginia! Do you think I'm stupid as well as blind? Do you think I don't know who my own team signs?"

"No, sir."

Walker turns back and watches the play on the field for a moment then flings up his arms in disgust. "Fishpaw is a drunken idiot. I ask for a player, and he sends me a field hand who can't put his drawers on straight!"

Some of the players begin laughing.

Walker turns around, his eyes strafing his players with contempt.

"I detect nothing funny here. It's bad enough I have to work with has-beens and no-talents, now I'm saddled with this! Sit on that corner of the bench, bush leaguer, and see what you can absorb of the professional game before I put your sorry rump on the next train home."

The other players slide down the bench away from Spottswood as though he is contaminated.

Walker's inaugural greeting aside, Spottswood resolves to prove his worth the way he always has: hard work. That evening finds Spottswood taking batting practice in the empty stadium as the shadows grow toward the infield. A bright light on the batter's box is all that remains of a once-brilliant day. Spottswood hits against a veteran pitcher, Joe "Lightning" Sellers, working between starts. The ballpark is cavernous, and the sound of ball meeting bat echoes through the empty seats. Spottswood hits everything Sellers offers.

Walker comes onto the field, drawn from the sanctum of the manager's office by the sound of solid contact of bat against ball.

"Curveball!" The deep tenor of Walker's voice sounds as though God is calling down a command to the Polo Grounds.

Sellers unleashes a curveball. Spottswood lunges and misses badly.

"Again!"

Sellers unleashes another curveball with the same result.

Not wanting to seem afraid, Spottswood calls his pitch.

"Curveball!"

Spottswood takes his already maniacal concentration up several notches. He digs in as Sellers unleashes, then misses the pitch by a mile.

Walker heads back into the shadows of the dugout and remains where Spottswood can't see him.

"Curveball!" The voice in the batter's box sounds confident.

Walker listens as the pitch thumps into the backstop.

"Curveball!"

The pitch thumps into the backstop.

"Curveball!"

The pitch thumps into the backstop.

"Curveball!"

This time the sound of bat meeting ball echoes through the empty park. Walker smiles and turns into the tunnel leading back to the clubhouse, his spikes echoing off the concrete.

Chapter Seven

TEST OF CHARACTER

THE NEXT WEEK sees little action for Spottswood save batting practice curveballs. The Giants embark on a road trip to Pittsburgh and Philadelphia, stopping along the way to play an exhibition against a local team in South Jersey.

Warming up, Spottswood feels at home, much more so than in the Polo Grounds. The field is ragged, and there are several gaps in the outfield fence, which are filled by people sitting atop their horse-drawn buggies. The men in the crowd drink; money changes hands freely. Players lounge in the dugout, except for Spottswood, who sits at attention.

After a few innings, one of his teammates—teammate in name only, since the veterans treat their new addition like a disease—a fellow called "Mudcat" Simmons, takes a seat next to Spottswood. Mudcat's face is lined, his overall demeanor aged and world-weary.

"I'll say this for you, Spotts: as tight as your ass is, there's no way a splinter's going to get up there."

"Shut up. Do you want Walker to kill me?"

Mudcat moves close to Spottswood and whispers.

"He's not going to kill you. He needs you to play center next inning. He uses exhibitions to break in rookies."

"I won't let him down."

"You're going to have to let somebody down."

"How's that?"

"These local peckerheads we're playing couldn't beat their own manhood. However, there's several hundred dollars waiting if they beat us."

"The game's fixed?"

"Have you learned anything the past week? They raise 'em dumb out in the fields."

"I wasn't raised in any damned field. And I don't gamble or truck with them that do."

"Relax, it's an exhibition. It doesn't hurt nobody, 'cept some rubes stupid enough to take a sucker bet."

"I don't—"

Mudcat presses a finger to Spottswood's lips.

"I'm not asking you to do anything. I'm asking you to do nothing."

"What?"

"Ole Henry's gonna serve up a couple not-so-fast fastballs your grandma could hit. When he does, don't break your splintery ass chasin' 'em down."

"I can't—"

The imposing form of Walker appears before Spottswood.

"If the ladies aid society meeting is over, I'd like Mr. Poles to position himself in center field."

Spottswood warily leaves the dugout, looking over his shoulder at Mudcat as he does. Mudcat gives him a wink and a nod.

The inning begins badly for the Elite Giants. A fat curveball rockets off the bat of an equally fat farm boy, and the lad chugs into second base as the ball is indifferently played in left field.

Ole Henry checks his defense, giving a surreptitious glance toward center, and glances at the runner on second base before going into his windup. He grooves a pitch right down the center of the plate, which the batter, an aging shopkeeper, wails to deep left center.

The left fielder, Tommy Sandifer, stands motionless for a second, but Spottswood has gotten an extraordinary jump on the ball. He runs further and further into left, his muscular legs picking up speed with each step.

Just before the ball reaches the wall, Spottswood pulls it in over his shoulder. After bouncing off the wooden wall with a sharp crack, he wheels and fires the ball to the shortstop, LeRoy Barnes. The fat farm boy has already touched third and is headed home. After a moment of confusion, Barnes steps on second base, shrugging his shoulders as he does, completing a double play.

The game is still in reach of the home team when Spottswood comes to bat in the top of the ninth. The pitcher, not knowing what to make of the new batter and assured that the game will turn out in his team's favor, launches his best fastball down the center of the plate. Noticing the defense is back, Spottswood drags a bunt down the first base line. He reaches the bag without drawing a throw.

Knowing their opponents can barely win, even with all but the most obvious help, subsequent Elite Giants batters swing wildly at pitches far out of the strike zone. Battling his own team's avarice, Walker gives Spottswood the sign to steal, which Spottswood obeys, easily stealing second and third.

With two outs and one strike on the batter, Walker gives Spottswood the green light again. Noticing the pitcher's exaggerated leg kick, Spottswood pushes off third base before the ball is out of the pitcher's hand. His right-handed teammate shields the catcher's view until Spottswood is almost at the plate. The catcher reaches for the ball, high and outside, and attempts to bring down a tag as the batter swings.

Like a streak of lightning splitting the sky, Spottswood shoots between the chaos around him and slides safely across the plate.

In the bottom of the ninth, Spottswood ranges far to his left twice to snag balls his indifferent and increasingly panicked left fielder refuses to run after. The third out is recorded on a strikeout by a batter frustrated that the deal between the teams has been betrayed.

As soon as the game ends, the Elite Giants, save Walker, bolt through the ballpark's exits and toward their hotel in the African American section of town. Decorum dictates that those in on the fix not acknowledge the deal has been betrayed, giving the Elite Giants a head start. (There is a vicious argument near the home bench between gamblers and home-team players with the resolution that the opposing team should be beaten or worse.)

Knowing they'd have to leave town quickly, the veteran Elite Giants pack their bags in advance and have them waiting in the lobby. Spottswood must dash to his room and heave his belongings into a suitcase. He spies his teammates sprinting in the distance as he comes out of the hotel and uses all his speed to quickly make up ground. Having some foreknowledge of what his players are up to, Walker has his bags already on the train and heads for the depot directly from the ballpark.

An angry mob of gamblers chases the Elite Giants, still in uniform, down the platform, throwing rocks and bottles as they go. The Giants hurl their suitcases through open windows in the last car and onto the platform at the back of the train.

The last man, Spottswood, jumps on the moving train just before the mob can catch him. Mudcat pulls him onto the train. It is not a gesture of compassion.

The players, Mudcat as their leader, pin Spottswood against the back door of the train car. The young player looks out into a wall of beefy men with scowling faces.

At his sides, Spottswood balls his hands into fists. A look of anger crosses his face. He is outnumbered but not afraid. "When I tell you something is fixed, it's fixed, and that's final!" Mudcat's words are backed by a chorus of assenting grunts. "Not only are we out a couple hundred bucks, but we can't come through here for years, if ever!"

Mudcat raises his fist to strike Spottswood, but before he can, he is flung backward. Walker now stands in Mudcat's place. The other players regard the scowl on Walker's face, which grows angrier by the second. They slowly disperse, some muttering under their breath as they walk away.

"I came here seeking the company of an honorable man for a drink. I guess you'll have to do, Mr. Poles."

Spottswood follows Walker down the cleared aisle as teammates find their seats. Eyes shoot daggers at Spottswood, but no one raises a hand. Mudcat turns and looks out the window as the train accelerates, leaving trouble behind.

Spottswood follows Walker into his Pullman Car. Walker reclines on the lower berth. For the first time, he seems at ease. Spottswood sits on the floor. Walker offers Spottswood a flask, which he refuses.

"Wish it was a habit I didn't have. But . . ." Walker takes a drink.

"Thanks for saving me." Spottswood's tone is sheepish.

"Saved yourself. We face tests in life. You passed this one."

"Thank you. Coming from you that means something."

"I'm just an old, broken relic."

"Fishpaw told me you played in the white leagues."

"That I did, my brother Welday, too—Toledo Blue Stockings of the American Association. But Cap Anson, a true peckerwood if ever one drew breath, got me and all other Negroes banned."

"Were you that good?"

Walker thinks for a moment, a brief flash of anger turning to disgust.

"Hell no. In fact, I was so bad that they banned us on the theory that people of our race couldn't compete with whites. I damn my inability."

"If you were no threat, why ban you?"

"You. He knew people of your ability would follow the likes of me. You, he couldn't compete with."

"How much have you drunk? I couldn't compete in the major leagues."

"That's what people like Cap Anson would have you believe. 'It would break the poor coloreds' spirits if we showed them how bad they were.'"

"That's what I've always heard."

"Don't believe it. I've seen a lot of major league games, and I've never seen anyone make a catch like you made today."

"Even if that's true, why would they break the ban?"

"Because they want to win. Men of wealth—only color they see is green. When a baseball owner wants to win bad enough, he'll go looking for someone like you. Be ready when he does."

"I can't hit a curveball, not consistently. Won't make it if I can't hit a curveball."

"We will have to work on that. By 'we,' I mean you will have to give me your undivided attention, and I will give you my best instruction."

Spottswood holds out his hand, and Walker shakes it.

"If only you knew what you've just done."

Spottswood can't decide if Walker is threatening him but reasons something good will come of their partnership.

Chapter Eight

A HARD LESSON

THE ELITE GIANTS' RETURN TO NEW YORK finds Spottswood at the Polo Grounds early in the morning. Walker stands by the mound with Mudcat. Spottswood and a catcher, Elijah Underwood, are at the plate. The light is diffuse and cool as sunbeams pierce the outer facade of the stadium. The grass glistens with dew.

Walker's voice reverberates off the empty seats.

"The secret to hitting a curveball is anger. It is a merciless, heartless demon. Since the serpent of the Garden of Eden, God has created no greater deceiver than the curveball. You cannot greet it as you would a woman on a Sunday promenade. You must judge the level of its deception and decipher where it will cross the plate. If it senses fear, it will eat you alive and send you back to the fields."

The last word pricks Spottswood's vanity.

"I was not raised in the fields!"

"Do not have the audacity to talk back to a curveball!"

Mudcat winds up and unleashes a curveball that Spottswood swings at wildly and misses. Mudcat smiles as Elijah tosses the ball back to the mound.

"What makes your heart angry, field hand? What makes it feel like it will explode and leap from your chest?"

"I was not raised in a field!"

Mudcat winds up and unleashes a curveball that Spottswood misses again. The sound of ball cracking mitt hangs in the air.

"What makes you angry? Is it the thought of your poor old mother scrubbing some white man's floor? Is it the thought of Massa . . ."

Spottswood feels blood rush to his face. "I come from honorable people."

"A sore spot. The field hand has feelings. We shall have to harness that anger."

Mudcat, clearly enjoying himself, despite the early hour, winds up and throws. Spottswood stands motionless as the ball pops into the catcher's mitt.

"I come from honorable people."

"The only honorable thing to do with a curveball is bunt it. Stick your bat out over the plate and bunt the damn thing since that is all you seem able to do."

Elijah returns the ball to Mudcat, now smirking as he goes into his windup. He throws a curveball that Spottswood calmly bunts down the third base line.

Walker walks off the mound in disgust, his cleats soon echoing off the concrete steps of the dugout.

That afternoon finds Spottswood in the heat of battle.

The scoreboard in left field shows the Elite Giants trailing the Providence Grays by a run. It is the bottom of the ninth with two outs and a runner on second.

Spottswood comes to the plate.

The pitcher winds up and unleashes a curveball that Spottswood massively misses. The pitcher then sends in another curveball that Spottswood flails at wildly.

When a third curveball wends its way toward the plate, Spottswood squares and bunts it down the first base line, easily beating the throw to first and moving the runner to third.

The next batter swings at the first pitch and pops it up harmlessly to right field. After the final out, Spottswood runs to the dugout where Walker is fuming.

"I don't need my best player bunting with the game on the line."

Walker throws a bat at the bat rack as he leaves the dugout. Spottswood stands motionless as teammates pass him on either side, some bumping into him with more than a little force as they pass.

Chapter Nine

A COLD INTRODUCTION

SPOTTSWOOD AND WALKER often share meals at a small restaurant in Harlem. It's a family place with a few small tables and potted palms. Being a typical evening, several children besiege Spottswood for autographs. He politely declines their requests.

"I can make my mark on this sheet of paper, but you'll just lose it on the way home."

"I would never lose your mark, Spotts," the voice behind the large set of brown eyes aches with sincerity.

"You say that now, but I know how things are lost in this life. The best things someone can give you come from the heart."

"Like what?"

"Like what I'm about to tell you. Never lie, cheat, steal, or drink hooch. Don't smoke neither. It will stunt your growth."

The child, a boy of about eight, looks Spottswood's compact frame up and down. "How much did you smoke?"

Spottswood gives the boy a playful swat on the behind. "Get on out of here."

Spottswood takes a couple of cheerful swipes at the rest of his admirers. The children run away.

"Nice dodge," Walker barely looks up from his plate as these words slide out.

"What dodge?"

"You know what dodge."

Walker notices Spottswood is distracted, looking at a very beautiful young African American woman who is dining alone in the corner of the room. She wears a spotless white shirt with a neatly tied black tie and a discreet black skirt, none of which can hide the fact she has an extraordinary figure. She carefully cuts each piece of food and places it on her fork gracefully. She takes small bites and chews each piece of her meal thoroughly. She reads Shakespeare's *A Midsummer Night's Dream*, contained in a leather binding, as she eats.

"I noticed her too," Walker stops eating for a moment as he contemplates the woman and Spottswood's reaction to her.

"Who wouldn't?"

"I haven't seen you chase women."

"Don't know if I could catch 'em."

"It's like hitting a curveball."

"You never let up. Maybe I just want one worth catching."

"Don't set your hat too high."

"That's the only place to set it. I don't want to be messin' with nothing common and low."

"She's neither of those. She's also not a woman for beginners."

The woman finishes her meal. She carefully places a bookmark in her Shakespeare, puts a black hat upon her head, grabs a small, black umbrella, and walks out the door.

"We'll see."

Spottswood tosses his silverware at the plate and yanks away the napkin tucked into his collar.

"The bill," Walker looks perturbed.

"After going 3-for-4 yesterday you owe me."

Walker shakes his head as Spottswood places a hat on his head and disappears out the door.

The street is crowded, as it always is—people picking up the ingredients of their evening meal as they return from work. Wagons and people clog virtually every inch of the street, but the woman moves through them effortlessly, as if guided by a higher force. Spottswood follows at a discreet distance at first, using his quick footwork and athlete's timing to dodge people and beasts while keeping his eyes on her.

At length, Spottswood moves closer to the woman. Just before he can tap her on the shoulder, she turns to face him. She plants the tip of her umbrella in Spottswood's chest.

"I don't know how it is where you come from, sir, but in New York only mashers and other men of ill intent follow women they do not know on the street."

"Then how will I ever get to know you? So I won't be a masher, that is."

The woman looks Spottswood up and down with a cold eye. "I thought you would have run at that."

"I only run on a baseball field, miss. I hope it is *miss*."

"I know where you run, Mr. Poles. You are quite a neighborhood topic of conversation."

"How is it right that you know me, but I can't know you?"

"I don't seek attention. Good day, Mr. Poles."

The woman starts to walk away. Spottswood follows.

"Miss, my intentions are honorable."

"As are most men's who follow women they don't know on the street."

"Miss, assuming it is miss, why wouldn't you want to know me?"

"Why would I want to know a baseball player who can't read or write?"

"But—"

"One or the other of these conditions would be bad enough. Together, they are positively repulsive."

"What makes you think I can't read or write?"

"Perhaps it's the way you dispense philosophy instead of your signature."

Spottswood points toward a brightly painted wagon.

"I can read. I can read that!"

The woman regards the wagon for a moment and allows herself a sarcastic chuckle. "I'm very impressed that you can read Italian. What does it say?"

Spottswood realizes his mistake and stops in his tracks as the woman walks away. When she is about ten feet away, she stops and talks over her shoulder.

"Mr. Poles, there are two types of people in this world: those who can't read, and those who won't. Which are you?"

Chapter Ten

SELF-IMPROVEMENT

THE ENDLESS MORNINGS at the Polo Grounds seem to wear on everyone except Spottswood. Mudcat throws curveballs, Spottswood flails at them, and Walker rains criticism on his star protégé. The day after his encounter with the young woman finds Spottswood in a decidedly different mood.

"How did it go with the young woman last night?" Walker's tone suggests he knows exactly how it went.

Mudcat sends a curveball toward the plate that Spottswood fouls down the left field line.

"Am I to take it from your silence that things did not go well?"

Mudcat throws another curveball. This time Spottswood times it and sends a screaming liner down the right field line. His face shows a level of concentration and anger heretofore missing from these tutorials.

"Why wouldn't she have you? Was it because you were a ballplayer who couldn't hit a curveball or a field hand who couldn't read?"

Mudcat throws another curveball and Spottswood hits a rocket back up the middle, barely missing Walker's head.

Walker knows a breakthrough when he sees one and doesn't let up.

"She didn't want to be seen with an ignorant field hand that couldn't write his own name!"

Mudcat throws another curveball. Spottswood lets out a primal shout as he gets all of it. The scream is punctuated by the sound of the ball bouncing about the seats in the right field bleachers. Walker and Mudcat turn to look at where the ball has landed.

The only sound in the stadium is the fluttering of pigeons frightened by the thunderclap from the bleachers.

The late morning hours find Walker in his office at the Polo Grounds. The room is little more than a closet in the bowels of the stadium. There is a small desk buried in a mountain of papers and one dim light bulb. Spottswood comes in and plops a large volume of Shakespeare on the desk, causing a minor landslide. Walker picks up the book and checks its heft.

"First you go after advanced women, now this."

"You have to teach me to read this."

"Why don't we go out to Coogan's Bluff, and I'll teach you to fly."

"I'm serious."

"So am I. The Bard is not the place one starts to read."

"Where then?"

Urged on by Spottswood, Walker buys several used children's primers. Their reading lessons take place at night, usually when the Giants are traveling by train. Such is the case a week later on a journey to Washington. Per the usual, Spottswood sits at the foot of Walker's berth with a copy of *McGuffey's Reader*.

"In Adam's fall we sinned all," the words come smoothly from Spottswood's mouth, his confidence increasing.

"Good." Walker's tone, a bit absent, is nonetheless reassuring and urges Spottswood on.

"A penny saved is a penny earned."

"Which later can be lost at poker."

"What?"

"We really need to educate you more in the school of life. Keep reading."

Spottswood puts the book down. "Do you think I could pass?"

"As what?"

"Indian, Cuban, somebody they would let into the majors."

"It's been tried."

"By who?"

"Me, for one."

"No!"

"After we were banned, a bunch of us formed the New York Cubans. We'd run around speaking gibberish."

"And?"

"People took it for what it was, a joke."

"Ever pretend you were an Indian?"

"Could never pull it off. But I knew a man named Charlie Gaines, second baseman, who did."

"How?"

"Found a son of a bitch who wanted to win more than he hated us. John McGraw, manages the Baltimore Orioles. Crazy man, started an argument up in Boston and kept arguing while they burned down the grandstand and half the city."

"What did he do with, uh . . ."

"Charlie Gaines. Said Charlie's name was Chief Takohoma, came from the badlands of South Dakota or some such. It worked until they hit Chicago."

"What happened in Chicago?"

"That's where Charlie was from. When they got there, his home folks had a big ceremony. Gave him a fine alligator valise. That was the end of Chief Takohoma."

"What kind of Indian do I look like?"

"One who tries to avoid his reading lesson."

"Seriously."

"Seriously, I had better never catch you doing such nonsense. You are an American, and in America people are recognized for their ability. Maybe not right away, but they are recognized. When your time comes, you will go in through the front door. And you won't wear any damned headdress."

Chapter Eleven

SECOND CHANCE

A FEW DAYS LATER, with a successful road trip behind him, Spottswood finds himself leaning against a street lamp, searching the large crowd that flows like a sea along the pavement. With a burst of recognition, he finds what he is looking for: the woman from the restaurant. Athletically, he weaves his way through the crowd until he is at her side.

"Grocery."

"Is that the new form of greeting? I really must keep up with the current slang."

"The sign over there says *grocery*."

"A child of four could tell me that by watching what went on there."

"H.P. Morton and Sons, fish and other edibles."

"That's a little better. Perhaps we should stroll down to the financial district to find out how good you truly are."

"I'd love nothing more."

"I was joking."

"I wasn't."

"I sense that, beyond your childlike façade, you're a very serious man, Mr. Poles."

"Where you're concerned."

"You don't know me."

"I knew all I had to the first time I saw you."

"That sounds like something from a cheap theatrical."

"That sounds like something that came from my heart."

"Matters of the heart are not something one discusses walking along a busy street."

"Where then?"

"I don't think there is an appropriate place where you and I are concerned."

Spottswood steps directly in front of the woman and blocks her path. She stops with an air of mild annoyance.

"Miss, I have devoted my energies to improving myself so that I could be worthy of you."

For the first time, the woman shows something besides icy indifference. "I'm flattered, Mr. Poles, but to be honest, a bit frightened."

"There's nothing to be frightened about."

"In literature, that's what the villain always says."

"I shall have to read about that."

"You shall."

"Can I at least know your name?"

The woman fishes in her purse for a moment and produces a card. Spottswood sounds out the words under his breath before daring to speak them aloud.

"Emma Dixon, E.L. Dixon Haber—, Haber—"

"Haberdashery. A little harder than *grocery*, Mr. Poles. Keep practicing."

Emma gently moves Spottswood to one side with her umbrella and walks away as Spottswood reverently holds her card, as if he's been presented a great treasure.

Chapter Twelve

A VOICE FROM THE PAST

THE STANDS BEHIND CENTER FIELD at the Polo Grounds, where Spottswood is playing, are full. In the background, there is the cracking sound of a bat catching good wood.

Spottswood gets an incredible jump on the ball and in a motion that seems almost effortless, hauls in a screaming line drive.

As he returns the ball to the infield, a voice booms out behind him.

"Spottswood!"

The area from which the voice is calling is engulfed in deep shadow.

"Spottswood Poles from Winchester, Virginia!"

Spottswood sets himself defensively.

"Spottswood!"

Spottswood turns his head back over his shoulder, obviously annoyed.

"Never disturb a man at his business!"

As Spottswood speaks, he sees Major Conrad calling to him from the grandstands. The major's form is caught in a streak of light as he sheepishly sits down. He stands out, being the only white face in a sea of African Americans.

After the game, Major Conrad makes his way to the first base dugout, where Spottswood signs autographs for a throng of fans. Spottswood motions with his head toward an usher, who guides Major Conrad to the locker room.

The evening finds the two at the table usually reserved for Spottswood and Walker. Spottswood can't help but notice that Major Conrad looks older, several streaks of gray working their way through his hair. Spottswood is surrounded by children, who depart one-by-one as he signs autographs.

"Apparently, being President Roosevelt's solicitor general is not as impressive as playing center field for the New York Elite Giants."

"It isn't as impressive as you think."

"I've watched baseball for about forty years; damned Sheridan's men played it while they occupied the Valley. I've never seen anyone play it nearly as well as you."

"Only little kids and old men care about what I do. No offense."

"None taken. The stranger I see in the mirror each morning grows more childish by the day. Who is it that you want to impress so badly?"

"You wouldn't understand."

As he speaks, Spottswood flicks the card Emma gave him over and over again between his fingers.

"Try me."

"A woman."

"Another area where I have sadly neglected your education."

"It seems as though we are in different worlds. She's educated, beautiful . . ."

". . . and you're not worthy."

"I'm not worthy."

"Look how far you've come, from Water Street to the Polo Grounds, and you're not worthy?"

"You don't understand."

"I understand that I have not done for you all that I could."

"How can you say that? You've given me a fine home, clothing, food, a sense of moral value."

"Moral value. Outside my home, I have let you and your mother be treated poorly. I should have insisted that the world see your worth instead of the color of your skin. I make bargains with society, political bargains, bargains with the past."

"None of which you can help. You are only one man."

"If one man is brave enough, that is enough."

"I know your heart."

"It always comes back to the heart, the subject where this conversation began."

"I don't know how to explain this. It's a feeling beyond words. A happiness when I think of her, a sadness. I can't explain."

"There isn't much in this world that I haven't seen or heard."

Spottswood takes a deep breath and looks Major Conrad in the eye. Spottswood's words rush forth. "I read to learn more to please her. I bought new clothes like I see the people wear on Broadway."

"Have you told her your heart?"

"I play harder every day so the headlines about me get bigger every day. It's still like I don't exist where she is concerned."

Major Conrad takes Spottswood by the hand, stopping his fumbling with the card. "Have you told her your heart?"

"How do I do that?"

"Poets have written volumes on the subject. I've found though, that if you forget what you're thinking, forget all the reasons it can't work for just a moment, and let your emotions speak for you, she will listen."

"That will work?"

"I did it once, and it lasted me a lifetime. Go find her."

"What about you?"

"What about me? You've seen enough of me."

"You came all this way."

"I'm your past. Your past will always be there when you need it. It is the future you must find. I'm an old man whose glory is long faded. You are a young man with a burdened heart. It is time you unloaded your burden. Besides, since my elevation in rank, Mrs. Conrad has decided I am fit for polite society. She is holding a reception at the Waldorf Hotel. I am told I will be the topic of interest at this reception, so, in the spirit of matrimony, I shall attend."

Chapter Thirteen

STORMING THE CASTLE

A SHORT TIME LATER, Spottswood finds himself before a large brownstone townhouse on the most prosperous street in Harlem. The exterior of the house is immaculate with two large urns filled with red geraniums softening, only slightly, its imposing facade. Spottswood rings the bell and a servant, Washington, answers the door. Washington, a thin, middle-aged African American, is dressed in a fine waistcoat with gray pants and spats. His high, starched white collar and black tie give him an air of discomfort, which he projects onto unwanted visitors, such as the one he now finds before him.

"Yes?" Washington's tone is firm and intimidating.

"Mr. Spottswood Poles to see Miss Emma Dixon."

"Is she expecting you?"

Spottswood produces the card Emma gave him, crumpled and torn from him rubbing it over and over in his hands.

"I hope so."

Washington examines the card.

"You could have found this in the street." Washington half flicks the card back at Spottswood in a dismissive gesture that indicates their business is finished.

"I didn't. I must see her."

"I can't."

"I'm sorry, I have to."

And with that, Spottswood moves past a man who is not easily moved.

His journey to the inner portion of the house is almost stopped by the opulence before him, rather than by the grasping Washington giving chase. The foyer is overwhelming: polished marble floors and walls covered with white-fabric wallpaper with gold inlay— every seam perfectly in place. Spottswood moves quickly toward the sound of voices in a room to his left.

A small group of people sit in a circle drinking tea. The furniture is large and overstuffed, the wallpaper red and of a textured fabric. There is a fine oriental rug on the floor. Everything is of the high Victorian style. Emma is to one side. Spottswood bursts into the room, Washington trying to keep pace.

"Mr. Dixon!" Washington's voice has an unaccustomed inflection of alarm.

"It's all right." Emma's tone is calm as she lowers her cup to a small plate on the table next to her. There is an awkward moment of silence as Emma rises and composes herself. Her father, a rotund man, absently polishes his glasses and places them on the bridge of his nose.

"I think some introductions are in order." Emma begins to motion around the room. "This is my father, E.L. Dixon. This is Booker T. Washington. He's staying with us for a few days after—"

"—making a speech at the Cooper Union," Spottswood finishes her sentence. "I read about it in the *Times*. It's a very great honor to meet you."

Booker T. Washington is a lean man with thinning white hair and a fine suit. He rises and enthusiastically shakes Spottswood's hand, a look of recognition passing over his face.

"And you're Spottswood Poles. I saw you Tuesday at the Polo Grounds. Went 3-for-4 off that tough left-hander for the Crawfords. Very impressive. Reads the *Times* too. Emma, if I were you, I wouldn't let this man get out the door without the promise of a social engagement."

"Actually, that was what I was coming here to do—ask Miss Emma if I could escort her on an excursion." Spottswood remembers to take off his hat at this juncture and holds it with both hands near his waist. He remembers that a gentleman does this so that his mouth, not his hands, do the talking.

"Splendid," Booker T. Washington is obviously pleased, much to Spottswood's relief. "A 3-for-3 off a left-hander and reads the *Times*, Emma. Very impressive."

"Yes, very," Emma's face blushes with a combination of embarrassment and rage as she focuses her gaze on the floor.

"Where were you thinking of taking Emma?" E.L. Dixon is finished attending to his glasses.

"Assuming I would like to go." Emma's words bear the inflection of anger.

"I was thinking Coney Island on Sunday."

"I've always liked Coney Island." Booker T. Washington is an unexpected and welcome ally.

"Assuming I would like to go." Emma's foot absently pounds the floor as she restates her case.

"Emma, I am tired of you devoting every waking moment to the pursuit of business. I think you would be wise to accompany Mr. Poles to Coney Island." E.L. Dixon proves judge and jury, finding in Spottswood's favor.

"How would one o'clock be?" Spottswood tries not to let the sound of gloating enter his voice. He knows too well how triumphs can be snatched away.

"That would be fine." E.L. Dixon looks down and begins polishing his glasses again.

Spottswood smiles broadly as Emma grabs him politely, but firmly, by the upper arm and begins escorting him from the room.

"Perhaps Mr. Poles would like to stay for some tea?" Booker T. Washington is firmly in Spottswood's corner.

Spottswood regards the tea setting. "A good cup of tea is something I miss from my home place."

Emma forcefully begins pushing Spottswood from the room. His token resistance makes it almost impossible for her to move him.

"I'm sure there's a training rule that Mr. Poles is breaking."

"Drinking tea? Drinking whiskey, which I don't by the way, would be another matter. Tea?"

Emma forcefully shoves Spottswood out of the room, practically falling over him as she does so.

"Say your good nights, Mr. Poles. I'm sure there's a craps game waiting for you somewhere."

Spottswood gets a quick last word in over her shoulder. "Don't gamble either."

Emma slips and slides across the marble floor as she pushes Spottswood toward the front door, which Washington holds open with as much dignity as he can muster. After much effort, Emma finally gets Spottswood to the threshold. There, Spottswood turns to Emma for what will surely be the most awkward good night of his life.

"The god of fools has smiled on you tonight, Mr. Poles." Emma fights to catch her breath.

"Now if only you'd smile, my life would be complete."

Emma slams the door, leaving Spottswood on the outside. He takes the crumpled card from his coat pocket, looks at it one more time, and tucks it in the breast pocket, patting his heart when it's in place. He flies over the stairs leading down to the street.

Emma storms back into the sitting room, face flustered as if she is about to explode. E. L. Dixon holds up his hand before she can say a word. "We have a guest. I ask you not to embarrass us."

Emma's rage is unleashed.

"Embarrass us? You just sold me off like an Oriental potentate dispensing one of his harem."

"It's only a trip to Coney Island."

"A trip I do not wish to make."

"Because you might have fun?"

"He is not a serious man."

Booker T. Washington interjects himself into the tense family dynamic. "You haven't seen him hit a left-hander."

"I have stood by for years and watched you turn away every man who has come to our door," E. L. Dixon's tone turns stern. "It's like you're waiting for someone to ride out of a Sir Walter Scott novel."

"He just might have," Booker T. Washington again takes Spottswood's side. "Don't underestimate the courage it took Mr. Poles to come here tonight."

"When your dear mother died, I promised I would raise you to be happy," E. L. Dixon's tone is somber. "There are times I feel as though I have not honored her final wish."

"I'll get nowhere here." Emma turns and stomps from the room, the sound of her dramatic retreat to the home's inner reaches marked by slamming doors.

Chapter Fourteen

CONEY ISLAND

THE SUNNY SUNDAY that follows finds Spottswood and Emma walking along Coney Island's boardwalk on a picture-perfect day. The sound of people having fun surrounds them. Emma is dressed all in white, magnifying her radiance. Spottswood sports a white suit with a new straw boater. Though they are jostled by those around them. Emma refuses Spottswood's arm and does the best she can to keep from touching him.

"So what shall it be, Mr. Poles? Do you want to impress me with some feats of strength? Maybe some light reading?"

"Why do you mock me?"

"Give me a good reason I shouldn't."

"Because everything I'm trying to become, I'm trying to become because of you."

"I've forced you to do nothing."

"You've forced me to do everything. From the moment I first saw you, you have forced my every thought."

"At least you're not going to die for my attention."

"Has that ever happened?"

"He said he'd die, but within six months he was married to someone else."

"Well, I'm not going to die, but I'm sure I wouldn't live happily without you."

"Mr. Poles, I don't know how things are where you come from, but in polite society we take things a bit slower."

"Society's plenty polite where I come from."

"And where might that be?"

"Winchester, Virginia, just below the Mason-Dixon Line."

"Then your family were slaves?"

"My mother was born to slaves."

"And your father?"

"Never knew him. He was a forbidden subject where my mother was concerned."

"And you let it go at that?"

"Any Southern gentleman would."

"Like your Major Conrad."

"Like Major Conrad."

"Did he have a wife?"

"She moves in a different social circle; spends time in New York and Newport."

"And you and your mother stayed with him?"

"My mother was born into his family."

"As a slave."

"We were never treated that way. Major Conrad has never made me feel like anything but family."

"Things are certainly different below the Mason-Dixon Line."

"How is that?"

"A musing, no more."

There is a long silence filled by the sounds of those having fun around them. Realizing she has overstepped, Emma resumes the conversation.

"What do you intend to do after you finish playing baseball?"

"Between you and baseball, my mind's fairly occupied. I haven't given it much thought."

"Games and women, that's not much of an intellectual résumé."

"Baseball's not for the stupid. Not if it's played right. Every pitch is a battle of wits between you and the pitcher. A step one way or another in the field can win or lose a contest."

"I wouldn't know. I've never taken an interest."

"Maybe now that you've taken an interest in me, you can take an interest in baseball."

Emma gives Spottswood an exasperated look and walks faster. Spottswood speeds up and matches her step for step. After a short while, the contest ends, and he offers her his arm. Emma takes it.

The day progresses as days at Coney Island do: the shooting gallery (Spottswood wins a large teddy bear that Emma promptly gives to the nearest child), the cyclone, eating hot dogs and ice cream, riding on the Ferris wheel, and the ball toss. At this last stop, Spottswood tosses a ball at a dummy at the back of the booth and misses high.

"That was impressive." Emma's words drip with disdain.

"I don't usually play in street clothes." Spottswood tugs at his starched collar.

"It makes that much of a difference?"

Spottswood takes off his hat, jacket, and collar and hands them to Emma. He picks up a ball and hits a dummy so hard that it takes out two others with it.

"It does."

Emma hands Spottswood his clothes, turns, and walks away with an air of indifference.

As night falls, Spottswood guides Emma to the attraction that pulls in almost everyone, the dance hall. The dance hall has thousands of white lights along the ceiling and is very crowded. The orchestra strikes up a waltz, and Spottswood leads Emma onto the dance floor.

"Do you know how to waltz?" Emma senses a potential embarrassment looming.

"No."

"Then what are you doing?"

"What I feel."

"Do you feel like looking foolish?"

"I could never look foolish with you."

With Spottswood guiding her, Emma blends into the waltzing crowd, and they become part of the swirling mass.

An hour of dancing leads to the need for some cool night air. Spottswood and Emma walk to the end of the boardwalk. Behind them is a full moon that casts a white light that looks like a river upon the blackened sea. Spottswood turns to Emma as she looks at the ocean, trying her best not to look at him.

"Why don't you smile? Do you know how?"

"I know how to smile."

"Couldn't prove it by me."

"I don't smile for just anyone."

"Then I'm just anyone?"

"I didn't say that."

"Your lack of a smile did."

Emma turns toward Spottswood.

"What do you feel when you play baseball in front of all those people?"

Spottswood becomes animated, his thoughts turning inward.

"When the crowd roars, your blood pumps until your heart feels as though it will explode. You can do things you only imagined you could do."

"I've never been to a baseball game."

"Never?"

"I never saw the point, although I'm beginning to see why you love it."

Spottswood strikes a batting pose, wielding an imaginary bat. "The sweetest feeling on earth is the ball leaving the bat. To feel every muscle in your body launch a ball toward the outfield. You see it leave the bat and then you're running without even thinking. As you run, you hear people yell. You can't really hear what they're yelling, but you know they're behind you. It's like they are suddenly part of you, and you have their strength. You can actually feel the noise moving through you like blood."

"Mr. Poles, you leave me speechless."

"Finally."

Spottswood pulls Emma to him and kisses her.

At first resisting, Emma begins to return Spottswood's affection, pulling him close to her.

Chapter Fifteen

THE CYCLE

THE COMING MONTHS feature several trips to Coney Island, more frequently featuring deep conversations and less attention to the attractions. These trips are far outnumbered by the evenings spent in the Dixon parlor. It seems that every African American of note passes through this stately room. Spottswood hears many schools of thought, some of which he finds offensive, and meets parts of society he never imagined existed.

Emma finds herself following the Elite Giants in the newspaper, when accounts can be found, and anxiously awaits Spottswood's return from road trips. She is not one of the common women who waits for the team at the train station, waiting for Spottswood to come to her.

He always does.

During the winter, Spottswood works part-time at the haberdashery. His notoriety brings in an expanded clientele. He also expands his wardrobe and adopts a heightened sense of fashion.

Winter turns to spring, and Emma finds herself in the left-center field bleachers at the Polo Grounds on a warm April afternoon.

Before the game begins, Spottswood trots over to Emma, who is sitting along the railing.

"Marry me." The words jump from his lips.

"We've only been courting eight months."

"Marry me."

"I don't really know you."

A helpful fan, Mary Kearney, a small African American woman with a newspaper, sitting in the seat behind Emma, butts in: "If I were you, I'd take that offer. They don't make them any better than Spottswood Poles."

"Marry me."

"Well?" Mary crosses the line between helpful and intrusive.

Emma turns to Mary as courteously as she can. "I'm under enough pressure here, thank you."

Spottswood seizes on Emma's words. "You want pressure? You have to say yes, but only if I hit for the cycle."

Mary slumps back in her seat and snaps the newspaper to attention before her. "You had her 'til then."

"What do you mean 'hit for the cycle'?"

Mary lowers her paper. "It means he has to get a single, double, triple, and home run in one game."

"Is that hard?"

Mary snaps the paper up before her again. "Impossible. In twenty-seven years of coming to the ballpark, ain't never seen it done."

"What do you say?" Spottswood leans against the railing with a feigned nonchalance.

Emma eyes Mary. "Twenty-seven years?"

"There's no way he can do it."

Emma sticks out her right hand, which Spottswood slowly shakes before releasing it with a kiss. "We have a deal."

Spottswood trots back toward the infield. Emma turns toward Mary. "Twenty-seven years?"

The top of the first goes smoothly for the Giants: three up, three down. Spottswood leads off the bottom of the first. He slaps the first pitch into the gap in right and legs it into a double.

Mary nudges Emma. "You're lucky he wasn't warmed up. If he was warmed up, that would have been a triple. The triple is the hardest to get."

Emma thinks about how fast the game is moving. There is no time to contemplate the magnitude of the bargain she's made. In the third, Spottswood looks at the first two pitches—both strikes—as if he is waiting for a particular offering. Overconfident, the pitcher throws an inside pitch that Spottswood turns on. The ball snakes down the line and hooks just inside the foul pole for a home run.

Mary nudges Emma. "Looks like love has put a little pop in his bat. Don't worry; he still hasn't got a triple."

The Giants have broken to a 6–1 lead. The game's outcome seems determined, but Spottswood's intensity remains high. In the fifth, he slaps the ball the opposite way. The ball heads toward the gap. Spottswood takes a wide turn around first, then heads back to the bag, where Walker is coaching.

"That was a double," says Walker.

"Already have one."

"Is there a rule against having more?"

"If it's that important, I'll steal second."

"If it's not too much trouble."

"None at all."

As the pitcher goes into his windup, Spottswood gets a huge jump and steals second cleanly. He's already dusting off when the shortstop fields the throw from the catcher.

Mary nudges Emma. "He's getting cocky. When a man gets that cocky, you'd better get nervous."

In the seventh inning, Spottswood goes with an off-speed breaking pitch and cues it down the left field line. He's halfway down the line to first almost before the ball leaves his bat. Walker hollers at Spottswood as he rounds first base.

"Stand-up double! Stand-up double!"

As he passes first, Spottswood kicks into a higher gear. He cuts past second cleanly, using the force generated by pushing off the inside of the bag to propel him toward third.

Mary gets out of her seat. "You're on your own."

Spottswood slides safely into third under a high throw. The crowd roars at his daring on the base paths. "Time!" Spottswood dusts himself off and carefully arranges his uniform. He then starts walking toward left center field.

Curious players from both teams follow him as he heads through the outfield. The crowd quiets from the uproar that followed the triple to a church-like silence as Spottswood strides toward Emma, his eyes focused, unblinking, on her. The seats around Emma clear as she stands and looks about anxiously.

Spottswood stands before her, then drops to one knee.

"I've kept my end of the bargain. Now, will you marry me?"

A disjointed chorus begins from the stands.

"Marry him!"

"Say yes!

"Marry him!"

Soon, half the grandstand is calling for Emma to marry Spottswood. The crowd is bemused at her predicament, an unexpected bit of entertainment. Emma looks around for someone to save her. At length, she turns back to where Spottswood is kneeling.

"Yes!"

Emma leans over the railing and falls into Spottswood's arms. The grandstand erupts in cheers as they kiss, and players begin slapping Spottswood on the back.

Walker breaks up the kiss and looks sternly at Spottswood. "If it's not too much trouble, we'd like to get on with the game."

Spottswood smiles sheepishly, turns and runs toward the infield with the other players following. Walker turns back to Emma. "I knew he was done for the moment he laid eyes on you. Don't ruin him."

Emma nods nervously as though she really doesn't fathom Walker's words.

Chapter Sixteen

DOMESTICITY

SPOTTSWOOD AND EMMA marry in the Abyssinian Baptist Church in a ceremony officiated by the Reverend Adam Clayton Powell Jr. Major Conrad brings Lucy to New York—her only trip outside of Winchester—and sits with her in the front pew (Adelaide Conrad, bowing to social etiquette, is not to be seen at a colored wedding). To Spottswood's surprise, Tom asks if he can stand as best man. Walker agrees to take one step to the right and serve as a groomsman.

Spottswood's time between April and October is all baseball. While the Elite Giants draw well in New York, they're a much greater road attraction. Spottswood's life is spent on trains to Pittsburgh, Indianapolis, Washington, St. Louis, and points west. While the major leagues end just west of the Mississippi in St. Louis, Negro League teams journey farther into the heartland in search of a dollar, barnstorming games between official contests help defer the cost of travel.

The newlyweds live at the Dixon home before finding a nearby apartment, although they are often in the Dixon parlor for lively political debates. Spottswood's absence has left Emma with time for political activities, including fighting for the vote.

Adam Clayton Powell Jr. holds forth at many of these gatherings, showing the oratorical skills and philosophical sophistication that will one day lead to fourteen terms in Congress. Powell eschews the separation of church and state, bringing the majesty he exhibits in the pulpit to common problems—sanitation, burgeoning rents, and economic inequality—that face his flock and future constituents.

As a local celebrity of some influence, Powell seeks Spottswood's approval, if not outright endorsement, of his efforts.

Booker T. Washington's place is taken by his protégé of sorts, W.E.B. Du Bois. Du Bois is the leader of the Niagara Movement, which seeks equal rights for African Americans. Educated at Harvard and the University of Berlin, Du Bois has a scholarly presence that intimidates Spottswood into silence. (He also is jealous of the way Emma seems to hang on Du Bois's every word. Sensing this, Emma is quick to hold Spottswood's hand when she feels him tense beside her.) Du Bois is considered radical in some circles because he opposes Booker T. Washington's "Atlanta Compromise," which states that African Americans will recognize the legitimacy of restrictions placed on them by Southern whites, in return for whites providing educational and economic opportunity.

Du Bois says the only way African Americans will attain equality is through the efforts of the "Talented Tenth," the intellectual elite of the African American community who will break down barriers and pave the way to opportunity. Emma counts herself among their ranks. Spottswood doesn't know where he stands.

Then there is Marcus Garvey.

Jamaican-born and a man of the world, having lived in Costa Rica and London, Garvey has become something of a cultural saint to the disenfranchised of Harlem. He advocates black separatism and, to this end, establishes various businesses, including shipping and amusement companies, employing only African Americans. These endeavors usually end in charges of fraud, something Garvey claims is the result of the efforts of Jews and white supremacists. Although he has never been there, Garvey pushes for the establishment of a nation in an Africa stripped of colonial rule that would serve as a home to all people of African descent.

As to who should be the ruler in this one-party state, Garvey gives more than a broad hint. He sometimes dons a military uniform with a fine-plumed hat, something Spottswood thinks would look at home in a Gilbert and Sullivan operetta. As far as his impact on the future of their race, Emma places Garvey into the category of entertainment and not one without social consequence or danger.

Garvey's Jamaican accent makes his views seem more exotic. His speeches rival Powell's for their forcefulness and appeal to the masses in a way Du Bois's intellectualism does not.

Sensing Spottswood's silence during Du Bois's conversations in the Dixon parlor, Garvey seeks to enlist him as an ally. "Brother Poles, can't you see yourself as the sports minister of a great African nation?"

Spottswood's reply never varies. "I'm an American."

Du Bois finds a far more eloquent ally in Paul Robeson, the Rutgers All-American football player and man of letters and culture. After graduating at the top of his class at Rutgers, Robeson earns his law degree at Columbia while earning his living singing at parties large and small throughout New York. He's hired by a prestigious law firm, Stokesbury and Miner, then promptly quits when a white secretary refuses to take dictation from him.

No sooner has this career opportunity been jettisoned than a new, greater career opens for Robeson. Struck by his physical presence and commanding voice, Eugene O'Neill casts him in *All God's Chillun Got Wings* and *The Emperor Jones*. Though not a trained actor, Robeson is soon the toast of Broadway.

Spottswood is awed by the seemingly effortless transition Robeson makes between athletics, academics, law, and the arts. In Robeson's oratory and philosophy, Spottswood finds a kindred spirit. Robeson says the extraordinary abilities of African Americans will forge "a new American spirit, leading to a greater openness of mind, a greater desire to do the right things and to serve social needs."

Robeson marries Essie Goode, a lab technician at New York Presbyterian Hospital. A regal, somewhat cold woman, she seems to manage Robeson's passionate nature and channel it into proper endeavors.

As he listens to Robeson speak in the Dixon parlor, Spottswood can't help but feel this is the kind of man Emma was destined to marry. The rumors of Robeson's infidelities fuel his imagination. He is more than a little relieved when Robeson departs New York to conquer the London stage.

Spottswood and Emma long to start a family, but it is not to be. Emma blames herself for this, but Spottswood doesn't. To him, she is enough to complete his world.

She is always enough.

Spottswood's other home in New York is the Polo Grounds.

A fire in 1911 destroys the wooden grandstand. The white owner of the National League Giants, John T. Brush, decides to build only the third concrete-and-steel ballpark in the major leagues. (Philadelphia and Pittsburgh construct the first two, something cosmopolitan New York can't abide.) Soon, a fifty-five-thousand-seat baseball palace rises from Coogan's Bluff.

Designed for the white major league Giants, the refurbished Polo Grounds couldn't fit Spottswood's game more perfectly. The playing field is a horseshoe with dead center 483 feet from home plate. Spottswood roams the vast expanse of outfield with speed not seen before in the majors or Negro Leagues. He awes crowds with his over-the-shoulder catches as he sprints back from his post in shallow center field, daring batters to hit balls over his head.

Few do.

The foul poles are as short as center field is long: 257 feet in right, 279 feet in left. Spottswood learns to hook pitches, especially curveballs, into the inviting right-field bleachers. He learns to slash balls into the curved sections of wall in front of the bullpens, balls that carom back wildly onto the field, confusing opposing outfielders and allowing Spottswood to take many extra bases.

With Spottswood as their leader, the Elite Giants play an exciting brand of ball that soon has their attendance rivaling that of their white counterparts.

Chapter Seventeen

MAJOR, WILL, AND JIM

A BRIGHT MIDDAY SEPTEMBER SUN is shining as Spottswood makes his way through lower Manhattan to 2 William Street, home of Delmonico's. A waiter wearing a long, white apron that covers most of his torso guides Spottswood past bustling waiters carrying huge plates of food and overflowing tables to a back room where serious business is done.

The year 1915 has been a great season for Spottswood, widely regarded as the best player in the Negro Leagues. The invitation to explore a "business proposition" intrigues him. Perhaps he's finally being recognized for his dominance on the field.

The first person Spottswood's eyes fall upon as he enters the small enclosure is Jim Thorpe. Widely hailed as "the world's greatest athlete" after his victories in the decathlon and pentathlon during the 1912 Olympics, Thorpe is playing a middling outfield for the New York Giants.

His real love is football. Thorpe's heroics for the Carlisle Indian School make him an object of national curiosity: can a Native American, raised and schooled as a white, shed his "savage" nature and become a model American? (Spottswood often thinks, not without bitterness, that such musings are never directed toward his race.) Thorpe is stripped of his Olympic gold medals for taking a few bucks playing minor league baseball. He remains something no medal can confer: a people's champion.

The amateur status of the world's elite athletes is reserved for those who can afford it, most through inherited wealth.

Next to Thorpe is Major Taylor, the cycling sensation who sets seven world records in 1898 and 1899 alone (earning him the title "The World's Fastest Man"). Retired and attempting a comeback, Taylor is a powerfully-built African American who looks far younger than his thirty-seven years. Like Spottswood, he is short with well-developed legs that strain the cloth of his pants at the thigh and calf.

Taylor first comes to fame during a six-day endurance race at Madison Square Garden in 1896. Only eighteen, he survived crashes, accidental and otherwise, to win several sprints within the larger race and finish eighth overall.

In Paris, he outdueled French cyclist Edmond Jacquelin and became a national hero of sorts. (An African American can become an American hero if national honor is on the line.)

Former President Teddy Roosevelt was a fan.

As they talk during the weeks to come, Spottswood finds much in common with Taylor. Like Spottswood, Taylor is familiar with white society.

Taylor's father, a Union veteran, is a coachman who works for railroad magnate Albert Southard in Indianapolis. Southard engages Taylor as a paid companion for his son, and Taylor receives an education comparable to the best Indianapolis can provide. When he sees how much Taylor likes his son's bicycle, Southard buys him one. It is soon impossible to ignore Taylor tearing around the streets of Indianapolis.

A difference between Spottswood and Taylor is the role of the dominant male figure in their lives. Whereas Major Conrad is a benign influence, Taylor's father is a bitter, driven man. He wears his Union uniform to the point of rags. When Taylor wins a race, his father's only observation is, "Why didn't you whip those white boys by more?"

Next to Taylor is another aging cycling legend, Will Slavin. A lanky man with an out-of-fashion handlebar mustache, Slavin is already on his second beer as Spottswood takes his seat.

Slavin is the grandson of an Irish immigrant who dies as a substitute for a wealthy patron during the Civil War. (The cause of death is dysentery. The place of death, the fine national Patent Office in Washington. Dying of a foul disease in an elegant setting is a very Irish death as Will sees it.) Like his father, Will seems destined to work in the foundries that dominate the mid-Hudson Valley until he marries fortunately. Carrie Taylor is the daughter of the middle of the three Taylor brothers, noted far and wide for their shotgun marksmanship. Retired from shooting, they open a hunting lodge in Suffern, New York, that is soon a fashionable haunt for the wealthy.

While working at the lodge, Will is introduced to the bicycle as a courier. Wealthy patrons soon notice his speed is better used on the velodrome track than delivering messages. A natural athlete, Will is an indifferent trainer known for his wit and amicable nature.

Slavin acts as Taylor's pacer in major races, making sure Taylor stays up to speed before a last dash to the finish. In a nod to blatant racism in some parts of the country, Taylor allows Slavin to win the odd race now and again. On American shores, an African American hero can be but so heroic.

At the far end of the circular table, a bit apart from the athletes and wreathed in smoke from an ever-present cigarette, is Damon Runyon of the New York American. (Runyon can stub out the truncated butt of one of his cigarettes, light another, and place it in his mouth without missing a puff.)

With Spottswood seated, Runyon, a short Midwesterner whose distinguishing feature is hair dramatically and symmetrically parted down the middle, begins laying out a proposition.

"Old Man Hearst is tired of the Kaiser. The Kaiser can only sell so many newspapers until we decide to enter this thing. So, he has decided to stage an entertainment."

"Freak show." Thorpe's tone is disdainful.

Runyon doesn't miss a beat in resuming his pitch. "Regret, first filly ever, won the Derby in May. Caused a sensation. So Ole Man Hearst figures we should stage a spectacle, kind of like in the Roman days, except without the bloodshed, of course."

"Of course." Slavin punctuates his remark with a slurp of beer.

"Hearst thinks a race—man, machine, and horse—would be a big attraction. Do it out at Aqueduct in Queens to kick off the meet in October."

"By 'man' we're not talking white man," says Thorpe, the tone of his voice bordering on contempt.

An awkward silence settles over the table as eyes turn to Slavin. "I'm Irish. I'm only considered white when there's work to be done."

Thorpe laughs, tension broken, and stares down at the napkin he weaves through his fingers as he speaks.

"My Indian name, Wa-Tho-Huk, means 'Bright Path.' Tell me, what bright path leads to running through horse shit as part of a freak show?"

"You took the money. Amateur status is gone," says Runyon.

"You can't be half a whore. Once you've done it for money, you have to make all you can before the public loses interest."

Major Taylor speaks up.

"Before I raced through the streets of Paris to entertain kings, I was doing stunts outside a bicycle shop in Indianapolis for people throwing pennies. Pennies add up. What Runyon is proposing is only a means to an end."

"What end?" Thorpe is clearly not convinced.

"I bought a house in Worcester, Massachusetts. Only Negro in the neighborhood. They accept me as much as they do because of my wealth. Runyon's right: people will pay and pay well to see the freak show he's proposing. When I raced, I knew people would root against me because of the color of my skin. A good many of them would turn out to see the Negro beaten and humiliated. I didn't hear their jeers. I thought only of the reward at the race's end. My motto is, 'My color is my fortune.'"

"There's more than pennies at stake here, fellas." Runyon picks up Taylor's thought. "Five hundred each just to appear and do some promotions. Two-thousand to the winner."

Spottswood lets out an unconscious whistle, tipping his hand.

"I can't earn five hundred in a year of racing anymore," Slavin chimes in. "Five hundred is the last payment on my petrol station in Sloatsburg. Your Whitneys and your Vanderbilts all stop there because their motor cars run low on petrol before they can reach Tuxedo Park. When they find out the man dispensing the petrol is one they used to watch at the velodrome, they're thrilled.

"Five hundred buys the station. Two-thousand coats the pumps in gold."

Runyon invites Spottswood into the conversation.

"What do you think, Spotts?"

"It seems like a mismatch."

"It's all science." Runyon has anticipated the question. "The horse must wait for the spur of the jockey. The cyclist must work his way up to speed. A man bursts from the starting blocks near full speed. People love this crap; man versus machine, John Henry taking on the steel driver."

"John Henry dies." Thorpe's tone is dark.

"Old Man Hearst promises to insure the whole thing."

"I'm not that fast." Thorpe returns to more practical thoughts.

"You're the world's greatest athlete," Runyon quickly retorts.

"I'm the world's most mediocre athlete. I do a lot of things— sprints, pole vault, high jump, javelin—half well. Champions in any of those sports could beat me easily."

"You're the name here, Jim—no offense intended." For the first time, Runyon looks around the table nervously. "Without you, this doesn't happen."

"No offense taken," Taylor chimes in. "Think logically, Jim. This is easy money."

"They took my medals for easy money," Thorpe looks at the floor. "There is no such thing as easy money, unless you're white."

Eyes again turn to Slavin.

"Only when there's work to be done."

Murmured agreements made and hands shaken, the deal is done.

The first promotion for the race will be Spottswood running a 100-meter dash at the Polo Grounds before a Giants-Dodgers game on an otherwise unremarkable Tuesday afternoon in September. Thorpe, who has declined to run, will serve as timekeeper.

When the day arrives, Spottswood dons unfamiliar track gear— he feels almost naked—and his baseball spikes. There are catcalls and derisive expletives flowing from the sparsely filled stands as

Spottswood takes his starting position on the foul line near the right-field wall.

Runyon holds the starting gun, and Thorpe, dressed in his Giants uniform, holds the stopwatch at the finish line. (Runyon has measured the distance precisely with a rolling measuring contraption he swears is scientific.)

Spottswood tenses as Runyon lifts the starting pistol in the air and is sprinting as the gun's shot echoes through the bleachers. Unencumbered by searching the sky for a ball, he concentrates on a sign—Canada Dry Ginger Ale—on the concession stand to the side of home plate. Muscles straining, lungs bursting, he flies by Thorpe and Runyon and has to circle up the third base line to get his legs functioning at anything approaching normal speed.

Thorpe glances at the watch, hands it to Runyon, and walks toward the Giants' dugout. Not having been timed before, Spottswood approaches Runyon with an air of curiosity.

"Two-tenths off the world record." Runyon stares at the watch, turns it over in his hand and reads the time again.

"Negro Wonder Among the Fastest on Earth" is the headline on the front of the evening edition of the American. It is the only time Spottswood's name will appear in that publication.

The day of the race is unseasonably warm and clear. Spottswood and his fellow competitors gather in the paddock as a carnival atmosphere of bands and cotton candy prevails in the packed grandstands.

Regret is a truly frightening animal. High-strung and huge, her handlers struggle to keep her subdued enough to get a jockey on her back.

Taylor and Slavin, accompanied by two young girls in fine dresses, look over their bicycles and make last-minute adjustments with wrenches. Taylor introduces his daughter, Rita Sydney (she was born during a tour of Australia). It is Taylor's wish that his daughter be educated at the Sargent School of Physical Culture in Boston. He sees her as a future teacher.

Slavin introduces his daughter, Velma Hate Slavin.

"She was the sixth of seven," he says a bit sheepishly after making the introduction. "Prudence, Charity, Hope, and Chastity were all taken. In the end, Hate may serve her better than any of them."

Thorpe stumbles in long after the others, a trench coat covering his Olympic uniform. He makes great theater of draining a flask before slipping it into his pocket with an affectionate pat.

Runyon, who is flitting about nervously, smoke trailing him like a passing locomotive, takes in this scene and sidles up next to Spottswood. "He knows he can't beat you," Runyon whispers conspiratorially in Spottswood's ear. "He's setting his excuse."

After a brief time, Runyon leads the competitors to the starting gate, speaking loudly and to no one in particular as he does so. "The race is not always to the swift, nor the battle to the strong, but that's how the smart money bets."

The starting gate is of the new mechanical type. Each competitor is placed in a small cell with iron bars running vertically across its front. When an attendant at the end of the contraption pulls down on a lever, the gate springs open and a bell rings.

As he takes his mark, Spottswood senses the tension on the bars before him, anticipating their opening. The bell sounds as though it is ringing behind him as Spottswood sprints down the manicured track. His senses heightened to an unbelievable level; he is alone as he leads the field at the fifty-meter mark.

Somewhere near the last quarter of the race, he senses Taylor coming up on his right side. Glancing, he sees the older man's face is a mask of anguish, gasping sounds coming from his lungs.

Spottswood slows, ever so slightly, not knowing why. Taylor crosses the finish line a fraction of a second before him, the charging Regret a close third.

Watching Taylor scoop Rita Sydney and the winner's cup—a large, garish creation—into his arms a short time later, Spottswood experiences a feeling he will know only a few times in his life.

Peace.

Will passes by Spottswood as he takes in the scene.

"The pumps won't be coated in gold, but commerce is served."

A short distance away, Thorpe is mobbed by fans. Any loss, be it of a race or medals, can't dim the popularity of the "World's Greatest Athlete."

Chapter Eighteen

LOOKING FOR C SHARP

A WARM, SUNNY SUNDAY AFTERNOON in September 1916 finds Spottswood and Emma walking away from the Metropolitan Opera. Dressed in fine evening wear, they have just seen a performance of Wagner's *Lohengrin*. The streets are bathed in the warm white glow of early electric streetlamps. The clopping of an occasional horse's hoofs sounds among the clanging of street car bells and the chugging of primitive automobiles.

"Did you like the opera?" Emma is always wary of taking Spottswood to cultural events.

"I liked what I understood."

"It was in German, which means you understood what?"

"You were there."

"We're married; you can stop trying."

"Can't stop trying where you're concerned."

"You'll wear us both out."

Spottswood drifts into a reflective silence. "I liked the part near the end where the music finally became whole."

"You were paying attention. That was a C sharp, the perfect note that completes the score."

"Too bad it took so long to get there."

"Anything of value in life does. What's your C sharp? The thing that will make your song complete?"

"You."

"Too easy. You already have me."

Spottswood looks into the distance. His face grows severe as he tries to give voice to a thought he has harbored deep in his heart. There is a long silence with Emma looking anxious before Spottswood speaks.

"To play in the majors."

Emma stops dead in her tracks. Spottswood moves ahead and strikes a batting stance.

"Why not?"

"Why not?"

"We talk about equality, but is that all we can do? I know I can hit any major league pitcher."

Emma looks at Spottswood for a moment, walks up, and takes his arm as they begin walking again.

"I'll bet you can."

The season winding down, Spottswood finds himself waiting at Grand Central Station for a train that will take him and his teammates to Cleveland. The New York Elite Giants laugh and converse loudly as they sit upon their suitcases on the platform. A white conductor, a solid man whose blue uniform highlights his red face, looks at them with disgust. Spottswood returns his stare as those around him grow quiet.

"Is there some problem?" The words jump reflexively from Spottswood's mouth.

"I'm just looking at you clowns pretending to be ballplayers."

"And what would we be?"

"You heard me."

"Are you saying we belong in the circus?"

"I didn't have to."

Spottswood gets up and starts toward the white conductor when he feels Walker's hand on his shoulder. "You're not going to change this idiot, not here anyway."

"Then how?"

"I've found a way."

The white conductor moves nervously away. The other players go back to their business, their former jocularity gone. Walker pulls Spottswood to one side. Spottswood watches as the conductor disappears down the platform. "As much as I hate to admit it, that idiot represents the average white man in this country."

"I wouldn't argue that point," is Walker's reply.

"How do we compete with whites in America?"

"We don't compete in America."

Walker smiles broadly and walks away, leaving Spottswood to contemplate his words.

Chapter Nineteen
HAVANA

UNBEKNOWNST TO SPOTTSWOOD, Walker has put together an African American all-star team, with Spottswood as the star attraction, to barnstorm through Cuba. At first, Spottswood is angry that his name had been used as collateral without his knowledge. His trust in Walker quickly dissipates this emotion, and the deal, as officially as such deals are consummated, is done. Spottswood and Emma, neither of whom has been at sea before, depart New York on a nondescript steamer. Leaving a dreary New York November behind doesn't seem like an attractive proposition when faced with an uncertain journey on the seas, even if it is only a few days in duration. The seasickness and questionable food of the early journey give way to a sense of expectation as warm sun hits Spottswood's face, lounging in what passes for a deck chair.

Havana is a revelation.

Brightly painted buildings set against a deep blue tropic sky stir even Emma's normally aloof soul.

Spottswood and Emma find themselves walking on a brilliantly clear Cuban afternoon; Emma is dressed in white linen with a parasol and wide-brimmed hat shielding her from the sun, Spottswood in a white tropical suit with a straw skimmer. Among the many races of people on the street, Spottswood and Emma move without notice. Sidewalk cafes are filled with American sailors and people dressed in everything from the finest clothes to almost nothing. Music escapes bars and restaurants behind the sidewalk tables.

"Let's move to Cuba." Spottswood's light-hearted musing bears a tinge of seriousness.

"The sun has baked your brain."

"The majority of people here are like us."

"Poor?"

"Negroes liberated this country from the Spanish. It was Negro soldiers who went up San Juan Hill before Teddy Roosevelt."

"Who got the credit?"

"Someday we'll do things so great they'll have to give us credit."

"You hit .406 last season, and I didn't see you get anywhere near the credit Ty Cobb got when he hit .369. He hit .369 with half the decent whites in the Federal League. He hit almost forty points less than you against a weak league."

"I thought you didn't follow baseball."

"I've developed a passing interest."

"In a few days, you'll get to compare us. Cobb is with a team of white all-stars, and Walker got us a game."

"Since when can whites play Negroes?"

"Since we're in Havana and some big shots want to see it happen. Walker is right. The only color rich men see is green."

"What makes you think if you play the whites, a Georgia cracker like Cobb will take the field?"

"He's in deep to some gamblers. If they say he plays, he plays. Now, what about moving to Havana?"

"You don't speak Spanish."

"I learned to read Shakespeare. I'll learn to speak Spanish. Besides, hitting a baseball is a universal language. If I hit like I'm capable of, everyone will learn to say 'Spottswood.'"

The innocent fun of the first days of the Cuban excursion give way to the deadly serious business of playing against Ty Cobb. The African American players look across the infield into the white dugout. On the top step, Ty Cobb sits conspicuously, filing his spikes. Cobb goes about his work with furious energy. Sparks literally fly from the metal, and their sharpened edges catch the sun in brief bursts of light. Knowing he's being watched, Cobb never looks up.

Horatio Jones, a young shortstop, watches Cobb's work with a sense of dread. "That has to be Cobb."

Mudcat regards the scene through veteran eyes. "He's just playin' with your head. He'd never actually spike you."

Walker watches the scene from a shadow at the end of the dugout. "Don't be so certain. There's nothing that crazy cracker won't do to gain an edge. You watch him; he'll let himself be thrown out stealing early in a game so that he can judge a catcher's arm. When the game's on the line, there's not a chance he'll be caught. There's nothing that stands between him and winning."

"Especially a colored man." Spottswood offers his opinion from further down the bench.

"Then I'm staying out of his path," Jones says this as much to himself as his teammates.

"What?" Walker's question is more of a statement of disbelief than a query.

"I'm not playing shortstop today with that crazy man coming down the line."

"The last time I looked, I was the manager, and you were the shortstop. I say you're playing short."

"Sayin' and playin' are two different things. It's not gonna be you in front of those spikes."

"But it will be your ignorant ass on the first boat home unless you go out to short in the bottom of the first."

Spottswood grabs Walker's arm. "I've got short."

The African American team is designated as the visitors—white teams always get last licks in such affairs—and Spottswood digs in during his first at-bat. Pitcher Harry Coveleski glares at Spottswood. Coveleski is a stout man with a sunburned face. Rumor has it that he's fallen in love with Cuba, particularly its rum.

Coveleski is already sweating a river and starts talking at a rate that matches the drops running down his face. "I'm comin' with a fastball. I'm tellin' you because you don't have a prayer of hitting it."

Coveleski throws, and Spottswood times the promised pitch perfectly, driving it deep over the right field wall. As he rounds second base, Cobb yells at Spottswood from the outfield.

"An uneducated ape could do that boy. That was raw strength, not strategy. When I come up, I will show you how it's done."

The first half of the inning ends with the African Americans leading 2–0. Cobb leads off the home first. He lets the first pitch go by as if it is beneath him to hit it. He spits tobacco juice on the ground before taking a couple vicious practice swings. Cobb drags the second pitch down the first base line for a bunt single. The first baseman moves noticeably out of his way as Cobb thunders across the bag. Cobb comes back to the base, shoving the first baseman out of his way.

"I thought we were playing the pride of the Negro Leagues. Looks like a damn bunch of school girls to me."

Cobb takes a long lead and dives back to first as Mudcat tosses over a pickoff attempt. He dusts himself off and turns toward the pitcher.

"Why are you throwin' over here? Nobody's gonna cover second when I steal it. You know I'm gonna steal it."

As Mudcat starts his windup, Cobb takes off. The catcher fields a fastball cleanly and hurls a perfect strike to second, where Spottswood is waiting for the ball. Cobb crashes into Spottswood feet first, his sharpened spikes tearing into Spottswood's right calf. In the same instant, Spottswood snaps the ball into his glove and tags Cobb across the face with a sweeping blow.

Cobb is knocked momentarily senseless by the impact. At length, Cobb jumps to his feet, a trickle of blood running from his mouth, and gets in Spottswood's face. Spottswood's muscles tense. He doesn't give an inch to Cobb, who momentarily looks confused.

"Don't even bother looking at the umpire, you ignorant cracker. You're out." Spottswood's voice is quiet but his tone authoritative. Cobb pulls back his fist, but before he can swing, Spottswood pushes him down on the seat of his pants.

"Next time, I'll beat your ignorant ass. Get off my field!" The last four words are said loud enough that those on the field can hear it.

With none of his teammates backing him up, Cobb gets up and slinks toward the dugout, a menacing glare offered over his shoulder every few steps. Spottswood flips the ball back to Mudcat. Realizing everyone is looking at him, Spottswood pounds his glove a couple of times and resumes his position.

At the end of the inning, Spottswood trots back to the dugout, trying not to show how badly his leg hurts, maintaining an even stride and firm pace. He sits down next to Walker after reaching the bench. There is a large area of red spreading across Spottswood's lower right leg.

"Bad?" Walker looks straight ahead.

"Worse than it looks. I feel blood runnin' into my shoe."

"Want out?"

"Hell no. He'll never have the pleasure of knowing how badly he hurt me."

"Have it your way, Spotts. Do me a favor?"

"Depends."

"If you get infected and die, leave me that nice new hat of yours."

"That's too fine for you."

"Emma?"

"I'll think about the hat."

As the next innings drag by, the dried blood on Spottswood's leg forms a red mass from his knee to his shoe top. Spottswood comes up for his second at-bat, noticeably favoring his injured leg.

Cobb yells into Coveleski from the outfield.

"Just throw him fastballs, Rummy. He can't run out anything; I've seen to that."

Coveleski, his face growing progressively redder and sweating more profusely, doesn't hide the anger he's feeling for his teammate. "Shut the hell up, Cobb. Anybody runs like you can't be running his mouth."

Coveleski's first pitch is aimed at Spottswood's head. As casually as he can, Spottswood leans back as the ball barely misses his chin.

"Quit screwin' around, Coveleski. He can't hit it far enough to run out anything." Cobb's bellow echoes throughout the stadium. There is mild booing and some catcalls coming from the stands, which only provoke Cobb to laughter.

Coveleski turns toward Cobb in the outfield. "Do you want to pitch?" The catcalls increase as the game's interruption by bickering teammates grows more frequent.

"I'm an everyday player, not an every-fourth-day pansy like you."

Coveleski throws a fastball, which Spottswood bunts expertly down the first base line. By the time Coveleski can retrieve the ball, Spottswood is already crossing the bag.

"Damn your fat ass, Coveleski! You are too slow to beat a crippled man. Do you want me to shoot the dumb son of a bitch?"

Coveleski glowers as he sets up on the mound. On his first pitch to the next batter, Spottswood steals second without drawing a throw.

"Boy, you stole that one on the pitcher. We've carried his fat ass for years." A short expanse of outfield separates Spottswood and Cobb. Spottswood can see Cobb's eyes, which present a hint of panic.

Coveleski turns toward Spottswood before the next pitch, faking a pickoff throw.

"He's got you, Coveleski. I guarantee you he goes the next pitch. Get ready at third."

Coveleski pitches from the stretch, but Spotts times his jump perfectly, getting halfway to third before the pitch leaves Coveleski's hand. Spottswood steals third easily, but slides hard into the bag, causing the third baseman to jump away as he fields the throw from the catcher. Standing up to brush himself off, blood again flowing from his leg.

On the next pitch, the batter hits the ball to left-center field, a high fly, not too deep. Cobb settles under it, talking as he lines up for the throw home after the catch. "Ump, don't let that cheatin' son of a bitch leave early. Boy, you best not run on me."

Spottswood waits a moment after Cobb catches the ball to tag up and race for home. He times his start so he uses the full force of the bag as a starting block behind his good leg. Despite the pain, Spottswood's strides are compact and explosive as he dashes toward the plate. Cobb throws a rocket. The catcher reaches up to catch the ball, but as he looks to apply the tag, Spottswood slides by him.

Spottswood meets Walker halfway to the dugout. The manager's calm demeanor is a stark contrast to the celebration erupting on the bench behind him. Walker motions for the other players not to celebrate too loudly.

Spottswood looks back toward left field, where Cobb stands silently. "Expected he'd be going crazy 'bout now."

"His silence means respect."

"Ain't mutual."

"Doesn't have to be."

As the Cuban sun sets in a brilliant orange hue, Spottswood finds himself lying on a bed, a Cuban doctor cleaning and stitching his wound. Emma winces as the doctor's needle goes in and out of Spottswood's skin.

"No matter how many times I see you injured," Emma says, shaking her head.

Spottswood waves off his wife's concerns. "Part of the game."

"A demon like Cobb doesn't play games."

"Neither do I."

Spottswood looks at the doctor. "How long?"

"Two weeks to properly heal."

Spottswood considers these words. "I'll only play the second game of the doubleheader tomorrow."

The doctor looks to Emma for support.

"I gave up years ago," she says, turning to go out on the balcony to admire the sunset.

Chapter Twenty

STATUS QUO

HAVANA OPENS EYES, but not in the way Spottswood intends.

Many white stars refuse exhibition games with African Americans for fear of their supposed dominance being exposed as a fraud.

Spottswood keeps hitting at a pace that defies conventional statistics, batting .400 at least twice. Scorekeeping is haphazard, and no one quite knows his true batting average. That the Elite Giants win much more often than they lose is the only thing that interests Spottswood.

Walker's fire turns into crankiness as he ages. The only player he does not regularly disparage is Spottswood. He bats Spottswood in the leadoff position to get his star the maximum number of at-bats. Once on base, Spottswood—who regularly steals sixty to seventy bases a season—is a disruptive force that knocks pitchers off their rhythm. Teammates' batting averages benefit from hurried deliveries and inattention to locating the ball.

The subject of African Americans breaking the color barrier is rarely mentioned, although stars of Native American heritage are routinely lionized. In 1915, Cleveland's American League franchise renames itself the Indians in memory of Louis Sockalexis, the first Native American to play in the majors.

"Chief" Bender, son of a German father and part-Chippewa mother, is the star pitcher of the dominant team of the second decade of the twentieth century, the Philadelphia Athletics. Bender wins seventeen games against only three losses in 1914 and jumps to the new Federal League for more money.

The Federal League briefly offers hope for those banned by the color of their skin from the established major leagues. Starting in 1913 as an "outlaw" league, the Federal League has outposts in Indianapolis and Kansas City, where players like Spottswood are known, and profitable, commodities. However, rather than revolutionize the game with African American talent, the Federal League's owners relish stealing established stars—Bender, Joe Tinker, Mordecai "Three Finger" Brown, and Hal Chase—off major league rosters.

After the 1915 season, the new league folds and with it any promise it holds for breaking the color barrier. Its demise leaves Walker fuming: "They'd rather fail than put a Negro on the field. If that doesn't sum up America, I don't know what does."

Players called "scabs" and "trash" a year before are welcomed back to major-league rosters. No such hand is offered to African Americans.

Ty Cobb continues as baseball's reigning star. Although he can't know it at the time, the Tigers win the last American League pennant of his long tenure with the team in 1909. He spends seventeen more seasons in Detroit, heaping invectives on foes and teammates alike. Rumors spread that he beat a heckler to death (some variations of the story have the man armless). Womanizing is more easily confirmed, but the laudatory press of the time ignores it. Harder to ignore are the rumors of Cobb fixing games. Eventually these rumors, grown louder than whispers, have Cobb exiled to Philadelphia for the last couple of years of his career.

Philadelphia is another puzzlement to Spottswood.

Every decade or so, the Athletics put together a string of world championships, only to have their owner/manager Connie Mack sell off his stars after pleading that he is unable to pay them fairly. Mack constantly says he is on the lookout for new and exciting talent. Had he really been looking, Mack would have seen a mother lode a few miles from Philadelphia's western border. Based in Darby, Pennsylvania, a team with the unlikely name—the Hilldale Daisies—is tearing up the Negro Leagues. Stars like Judy Johnson at third base, Oscar Charleston in center, and catcher Louis Santop are the equal to any of their major-league counterparts.

Walker, who knew Mack as a catcher with Washington and Pittsburgh before the turn of the century, is not surprised at Mack's reluctance to sign African Americans. "Connie's not a bigot; he's smart. They call him 'the great strategist.' A great strategist rarely makes the first move. They let someone else make the first move, take the grief, then react to their advantage.

"The first move is always made by the most emotional man, not the smartest."

Abe Rothstein and his son, Aaron, who succeeds him as the owner of the Elite Giants, are definitely smart, if somewhat emotional, men. During their rare business dealings with Spottswood, the Rothsteins mention frequently that they understand the frustrations of African Americans who want to play in the majors.

Jews are banned from the trappings of white American power—politics, country clubs, and the ownership of major league baseball teams to name a few. By setting up an alternate economy in which they and their African American employees can thrive, the Roth-steins argue that they are doing the best they can, given the conditions.

Clothiers by trade, the Rothsteins make sure their players are the best dressed, if not best paid, players in the league.

The façade of prosperity for all is maintained.

Chapter Twenty-One
DUTY

SPOTTSWOOD READS A NEWSPAPER with reports about America's involvement in World War I on the front page. Emma is clearing the table. Spottswood lays the paper aside with great gravity. Emma looks at him quizzically.

"Think I'll enlist."

"Think I'll sprout wings and fly to New Jersey."

There is a long silence. Emma says, "This is where you say, 'If I had wings, I'd fly somewhere a lot better than New Jersey.'"

"I'm serious."

"What would the Army want with a man your age?"

"If I was aging in human years, nothing. I age in baseball years."

"How old does that make you?"

"I've been telling 'em twenty-three for four years. Before that, I was twenty-one for three."

"We're talking about the reality of you being older. You're too old to go to war."

"I stole sixty-one bases last season. Show me anyone twenty-two, twenty-three who can do the same."

"Nobody in France is outrunning bullets."

"Cobb is enlisting."

"Maybe they'll let you share a tent."

"Maybe they'll let us share a ball field if I come home a hero."

"Is that what they'll do? Don't you remember those poor colored soldiers who went up San Juan Hill before Teddy Roosevelt? Where did that get them?"

"They lacked my talent."

"A lot of them ended up lacking their life."

"If colored men fight well in France, they will have to recognize us as equals. That includes playing in the major leagues."

"How long have you been saying this? 'If I just work harder, if I'm that much better, they'll have to let me in.' They are never going to let you in, no matter what you do or how good you are. That is reality. You're already the best player in the country, and where has it gotten you?"

"It's about to get me to France."

"I won't be here when you return."

"You will."

"I'll leave."

"All you told me about was other women. You didn't say anything about Germans."

"I have put up with your life on the road. Just because I told you about other women doesn't mean you listened."

"I did more than listen. I lived by your wishes and my word." There is more than a hint of anger behind Spottswood's pronouncement.

"My wishes? I wanted you off the road years ago."

"And how would we live?"

"Like a normal married couple."

"You knew the day I met you that I wasn't normal. I certainly knew you weren't."

"Then what are we?"

"We're better. We've been given talents that let us transcend restrictions."

"Try telling that to any waiter outside New York. Tell that to the desk clerk who makes you go to another part of town because he won't rent you a room. To them you're just another nigger."

Spottswood sits dead silent for a moment, anger brewing just below the surface. He holds up his hand, as if to deflect Emma's words and hold back his own, then speaks deliberately, choosing his words carefully.

"I hate that word, and I hate that I would hear it come out of my wife's mouth."

"Better from me than some white bastard trying to break you; see reality."

"I see my reality in France."

"I have gone along and looked away when I've had to. I cannot do either now."

"I need you behind me, but I will do this without you."

"Yes, you will."

Spottswood is silent for a moment. The newspaper is snapped to attention before him as the flimsiest of shields. The words flow more quietly from his mouth after a long silence.

"Tom is going to France. His National Guard unit has been activated."

"Let him. It's a white man's war."

"I really have no choice in this."

"You have a choice, and you are not choosing me."

Emma roughly puts the last of the dishes in the sink, grabs her coat and hat, and departs out the front door, slamming it after her.

Spottswood drops the newspaper to his lap and stares into nothingness.

Chapter Twenty-Two

CAMP

AS HE LOOKS AROUND THE TRAIN PLATFORM, new recruits boarding, Spottswood starts to see the wisdom of Emma's words. Those surrounding him are much younger; they bubble with an energy he no longer possesses. Emma's words reverberate through his head as though she were standing in front of him. She is not. Emma goes to her father's home several days before Spottswood's induction. When Spottswood visited, Washington, now stooped by age, informed him that "Miss Emma" was not at home. Spottswood did not consider assaulting the castle as he once did. Washington's eyes now lack the resolve with which he once turned the unworthy away from this door. Spottswood didn't know if this was sympathy or infirmity. His question was answered when he felt Washington's hand grasp the back of his shoulder as Spottswood turned to go down the steps of the brownstone for what he hoped would not be the last time.

"Please, sir, be careful. Take care of yourself."

Leaving New York, the train plunges night and day southward. Spottswood knows this route well from years of road trips. However, the train crosses his personal frontier as it moves through Bristol, Virginia, into Bristol, Tennessee. As he watches through the darkness at the transition, Spottswood wonders how two states—in this case, on opposites sides of the street—can be so different. How do men allow themselves to be divided artificially, not only by non-existent geographical boundaries, but by invisible walls of hatred?

The train rumbles on, letting its occupants outside to stretch only after long intervals, until it reaches Alabama.

Major Conrad spoke about his Confederate comrades almost as family through the years. Alabamans were clearly the bastards of that family. Major Conrad was awed by their ability to take and inflict punishment, but inferred this was due to a lack of intellect rather than presence of superior will.

The air is thick with summer humidity as Spottswood, in the uniform of an Army sergeant, moves across the drill field. In the background, a unit of African American soldiers goes through marching and combat drills. Spottswood steps into the tent of Major Hamilton Fish, the unit's white commander (no African American is allowed to attain a rank higher than sergeant).

Hamilton Fish is a tall, muscular man, a recent All-America football player at Harvard. Spottswood snaps off a crisp salute, which Fish casually returns.

"The great Spottswood Poles." The words come out warmly in Fish's deep baritone.

"Sergeant Poles will do, sir." Spottswood looks about in embarrassment.

"I hate to be that formal with someone whose skills I admire, but I can't let you call me 'Ham,' like they did back at Harvard. Wouldn't look right."

Spottswood stifles a laugh.

"Something funny, sergeant?"

"You just lost me a dollar."

"How so?"

"Captain Broy with the Georgia regiment yonder said you'd mention you went to Harvard less than a minute after we met."

"Broy—Yale man. If I went to Yale, I wouldn't mention it at all."

"Yes, sir."

"Any other ways in which I can enrich Captain Broy?"

"He said you'd mention about playing football."

"I was an All-American end at Harvard, damn proud of it. As a matter of fact, that's how I met Paul Robeson from Rutgers. Wonderful player, credit to the Negro race—also had the most wonderful singing voice. When they offered me a colored unit, I naturally thought of Paul."

"Naturally."

"Even though you're no longer the great Spottswood Poles, you remember how to swing a bat, don't you?"

"Old habits die hard, sir."

"Yale men die harder. It just so happens that I would like to get up a baseball game with Captain Broy's unit. Think you could be of some assistance?"

"Know I could."

"We'll see what we can do about getting back that dollar."

The game is played on a blazing-hot Alabama afternoon. Spottswood finds himself managing and batting leadoff against a Georgia team fielding several minor leaguers. The game is tied 3–3 in the ninth with runners on second and third with one out for the Georgians, who have last licks.

One of the Georgians hits a screamer to center, which Spottswood fields cleanly on the fly. The runner on third tags and heads home. Spottswood's throw is right on the money, nailing the runner by a good ten feet. The umpire, who is white, calls the runner safe. The Georgians celebrate, while the African American troops, led by Major Fish, argue with the umpire.

"How could he be safe?" Fish's sunburned face is turning purple with rage.

The umpire turns his back while uttering a reply. "Game's over. I call 'em as I see 'em."

"You didn't see that one!"

Spottswood, who has run in from center, pulls Fish away from the argument. "This isn't a Harvard debate. You're arguing against a bunch of whites in Alabama."

"Right is right."

"Not in Alabama."

Spottswood leads Fish away. The Georgians taunt and jeer. The looks on the faces of the African American troops are a mixture of frustration and anger. Some clench their fists, but soon think better of it.

That night finds Spottswood alone in his tent reading a letter from Major Conrad. He has gotten a letter from the head of his former household each week since leaving New York.

Spottswood is stunned by the words before his eyes.

"As I reach the end of my days, I have time to reflect on all I have done and on that I should have done. I fought well for a bad cause, a cause that masked its evil behind the cloak of Constitutional law and social convention. I surrendered myself to such conventions at the cost of hiding my great love from the world. People who know my heart—you and your mother—are, by convention, separated from me. If it is enough, know that I have, and always will, consider you a son. Should we not meet again in this life, know that your mother and I will be waiting for you in a place where none judge or are judged and only love abides."

As Spottswood contemplates the letter, an African American private runs up to the tent. Before he can say anything, Spottswood salutes. The private regains his composure somewhat, salutes, then begins speaking in an excited manner. "Sarge, a bunch of the boys are headed down to the creek to settle up with them crackers what cheated us today."

Spottswood jumps off his cot, pulls on his pants, grabs his boots, and heads into the night. Running and shoving his way through a mass of men moving with angry purpose, Spottswood arrives at the creek before any real damage has been done. White troops line up along one side of the creek, African American troops along the other. They are exchanging foul words and dirty looks. No blows have been thrown.

"You coons can't lose like men," a white sergeant lets loose this invective to murmuring approval behind him.

"You can't win like men," an African American corporal shoots back. "You just can't stand that we're better than you."

"Come over here and say that."

The African American corporal jumps into one side of the shallow creek and the white sergeant the other. They are just beginning to fight when Spottswood separates them, knocking both into the water. The white soldier reacts angrily.

"Get your filthy hands off me, nigger!"

A shot rings out from the creek's bank, and the soldiers—near riot moments before—fall silent. For a moment, all that can be heard is the shot echoing through the woods and the flapping wings of startled birds. Major Fish replaces the safety on the large revolver he's holding with a distinct click, a foreboding sound.

"That's Sergeant Poles to you, soldier. Strike him, and I'll shoot you dead."

Captain Broy appears and with some difficulty pushes his way through his troops. He is a thin, pale man with a flamboyant shock of blond hair. "What idiot fired that shot?"

"The idiot that was here to control your troops," Fish's voice is deep and resonant.

"Fish, are you insane?"

"Aren't you forgetting something, captain?"

Broy awkwardly salutes. After a long moment, featuring Broy's hand trembling against his forehead, Fish returns it.

Thus acknowledged, Broy resumes his line of questioning. "Begging the major's pardon, but is the major insane, sir?"

"Maybe insane enough to shoot a Yale man whose scum of a unit cheats at baseball."

There is muffled laughter from the African American troops.

"Begging the major's pardon, but that is not funny, sir."

"It wasn't meant to be, captain. Take your unit and get them back to camp."

The soldiers on both sides of the creek stagger back to camp, some mumbling. Fish stops Spottswood, who is among the last to leave.

"In the future, I'd appreciate it if you'd tell your commanding officer before taking such action."

"I thought I could handle it, sir."

"You almost handled getting my best noncom killed."

"Sorry, sir."

"Sergeant, do you not trust me because I'm white?"

"Sir?"

"Speak freely."

"No, sir, no such thing ever crossed my mind."

"Rest assured, it has never crossed mine. I will always stand by my troops."

The remaining weeks of training passed without open hostility between the races. The new troops focus their attention on beating the Hun, but at times their training to do so seems laughable. Rifles are in short supply, and soldiers train with wooden replicas while others practice with the limited ammunition available on the firing range. Sawdust dummies are stabbed with bayonets until their yellow blood spills over the red Alabama clay. Flour bombs are hurled at troops, creating coughing fits as white clouds cover mock battlefields.

White troops are trained in the art of using gas masks.

There aren't enough for the African Americans.

Chapter Twenty-Three

PASSAGE

FINALLY, THE DAY COMES. Spottswood's unit is put on a train for the embarkation point, Norfolk. As Spottswood smells the salty air, he remembers the early misery of his voyage to Cuba. He knows he will have to hide any signs of seasickness from the younger troops; a role model can't maintain that status while puking in a bucket.

The quarters given the troops for passage make a tramp steamer look like a floating palace. There is some dark humor about a U-boat attack being preferable to enduring such conditions.

The soldiers in Spottswood's unit swing in their hammocks below decks. The hammocks sway back and forth with the rolling of the sea. The ship's hull creaks and sighs. The lights in this dank confine flicker on and off with the motion of the ship, staying on only when it is totally level, which isn't often.

Major Fish strides into the narrow aisle between the hammocks, which stretch three-high toward the deck above. Spottswood is the first to see Fish. He jumps to his feet and snaps to attention.

"Atten-tion! Commanding officer on deck!"

Troops try to get out of their hammocks. Some land on their feet;

others tumble awkwardly to the floor, getting upright as quickly as they can. Fish lets the scene before him play out a bit before addressing the serious news that has brought him below deck.

"As you were, men! I've received our orders from AEF headquarters. We will be assigned to French command for combat purposes."

There is a general groan and muttered complaints from the troops. Spottswood grasps his role immediately. "Order in the ranks!"

After the murmuring dies to silence, Fish resumes.

"I know you're disappointed, but we cannot act as anything less than the soldiers we've trained to be."

A voice, emboldened by the darkness, rings out. "Are they sayin' we ain't good enough?"

Rather than call out the questioner, Fish replies. "It's not what they say, it's what we know. We are the best unit in the AEF. Some say things like that, others prove it. We will prove it on the battlefield no matter whose flag we fight under."

"Does this mean our own generals don't want us?" another voice from the darkness is heard.

"It means the French want us more. We will fight wearing their helmets and ordinance."

Fish turns and walks away into the darkness. The groaning and angry mumbling grows. Spottswood steps to the center of the aisle and looks about him. The flickering lights play off his face as he speaks.

"Are you going to let this break your spirit?"

"They're sayin' we ain't fit to serve with white men!"

"They've got it backward! They're afraid to serve with us! The French are in the thick of it. They need men, good men! They need us. We will fight so goddamned hard, men will weep at the stupidity of not having us fight alongside our countrymen. When I play baseball, I wear a different uniform than the men who are in the major leagues—men who say they are my superiors but who know they are not. I never disgrace my uniform no matter what uniform I'm wearing. I play where they let me play because I have to. But one day, I will play where I want to play because they will see my worth is so great that they can't ignore it. That is what we have to do now. We don't have to like it, but we have to do our duty as our duty is assigned. But know the generals that did this will regret the day they turned their backs on the 369th Infantry Division. We will have to fight harder and longer to earn our place. I guarantee you, the day we march into Berlin, we will be at the head of the column."

There are quiet grunts of assent as Spottswood speaks. He then slides back into his hammock, and the ship goes quiet save for the creaking of its hull.

Chapter Twenty-Four
ALONE

LIKE ALL THE STORES AROUND IT, Dixon's Haberdashery sports patriotic posters in its windows: white faces urging bravery to protect white women and children from the Hun, a spike-helmeted menace always portrayed as coal black. Emma tells herself that the caricature doesn't matter. All that matters is the red, white, and blue bunting that surrounds the poster's edge. Her feelings of patriotism, however, are subservient to those of betrayal, loneliness, and loss. Emma Dixon would never be in the thrall of any man; that's what she always told herself.

She has failed.

Worse, Emma feels she has failed Spottswood. Pride—and the inadequacy of words in such situations—leaves her in a depressed silence.

She folds an order of new pants as her father comes up beside her. He has grown gray and stooped.

"You don't have to be here all day, every day."

"Where else would I be?"

"Concerts, plays."

"Not alone. It doesn't look proper."

"It's just as though he were on a road trip."

"You know he's on no damned road trip."

"Language! Spottswood has always had something to prove. Some people have a talent, a higher calling that demands they take action."

The folding stops.

"And where do I fit into that higher calling? When will he know he's fulfilled his destiny?"

"He'll know. You both will."

"I don't know if I can stand this much longer."

"You can say that to me, but never admit it to yourself. Sometimes we have to utter our fears to face them."

Emma starts to cry, and her father wraps his arms around her. Emma disintegrates into sobs as her father silently holds her.

Unfolded pants fall to the floor.

Chapter Twenty-Five

FRANCE

THE BOXCAR IS A RICKETY AFFAIR, with wide spaces between its slats that let gray day seep in. It's not raining; the sky is simply joyless.

In the distance, artillery can be heard. The boxcar is rolling through the outskirts of Paris, taking Spottswood's unit to the front. Spottswood and his fellow soldiers lie on the dusty floor in varying states of discomfort.

Carved on the enclosure's walls are words in English and French, left by previous occupants. Some mark the dates soldiers passed through. Others are obscene. There are cartoons, but nothing like Spottswood saw in the funny papers. Even by the standards of ball-players, they are filthy—a very low bar, uncleared. Looking at the English messages, Spottswood is just glad he doesn't read French.

One of the soldiers, Earnest Chambers, nudges Spottswood, who is half reading the *Odyssey* through sleep-deprived eyes. (He feels deeply for the plight of Ulysses and Penelope. How little the basics of human emotion change through the course of the centuries.)

"Sarge, is that what I think it is?" Chambers points through a particularly large hole in the boxcar wall.

Spottswood clears his eyes and sits up. Through the moving slats, he catches glimpses of the Eiffel Tower. He places Emma's worn card in *The Odyssey* as a bookmark.

"It certainly is."

"Gay Pair-ee."

"As long as I was being stupid, Emma told me to see Paris."

"Seen enough?"

"Reckon so."

Spottswood looks back down at his book.

"How desperate are they calling us to the front?" Chambers face betrays his anxiety.

"You know it's desperate when they call Negroes 'men.'"

Chamber struggles to put on his gray French helmet, which is much heavier than its American counterpart. Spottswood puts his book aside and places the helmet firmly on Chambers head, adjusting the chin strap.

"Thinkin' of what it's gonna be like?" says the newly armored Chambers.

"Not really."

"You're not afraid of dying?"

"What more do I have to live for? I've seen Paris."

When the Eiffel Tower moves from view, it is replaced by the image of a hospital train on the next track over. Orderlies carry the dead and wounded from the overflowing passenger cars. On the last car, orderlies toss helmets and other discarded battle equipment into the back of an open truck. Small children run off with a couple of helmets and some rations as orderlies give half-hearted chase.

Spottswood looks down at his worn, dented helmet. Who has worn it before, and was the former owner among the living? He also muses that the helmet offers much more protection than the inverted soup saucer worn by American troops. In making the African American troops separate from their countrymen, the upper echelon has given them a protective advantage.

The evening finds the 369th ending its train journey two miles from the front. Ordinarily, being this close to the action would constitute imminent peril. But the lines between the Germans and French have moved only a matter of yards during the preceding two years. Ordered to sleep, the bodies that compose the 369th don't obey. Instead, they watch a night-long bombardment through half-shut eyes. Fish notes that an artillery display of this magnitude almost certainly means a major offensive push in the morning.

Just before dawn, the order comes to move out. Packs and rifles are slung into position as the ranks form. Breakfast is bread and water on the march.

Spottswood's unit marches warily toward the front. Stray bullets whiz over their heads, and the ground shakes from the impact of artillery shells. Soldiers lose their cadence as they look to the side of the road. There are several freshly dug graves marked by upturned rifles, their bayonets buried in the earth with American helmets hung from their stock. Spottswood gets the soldiers back into line quickly.

A group of French officers pull up in a large touring car. They are spit-polished shiny and officious. They barely regard the American troops marching before them. Among the officers is a tall, muscular American officer, who towers above his counterparts. The French officers and lone American climb a small hill to an observation bunker. It is surrounded with sandbags on every side, obviously the most secure spot in the area.

Spottswood and his African American comrades wear the uniform of the 369th Infantry Division Hellfighters. They have khaki

American uniforms, accented by gray French helmets and gear.

The battlefield is a wide expanse of hell, pockmarked with shell holes and crisscrossed with barbed wire. An American unit is stumbling back from an attack under the watchful eyes of the French officers. The unit is Captain Broy's. Many of the soldiers are wounded or shell-shocked by their first action. Some run frantically back to the safety of the trenches, diving in head-first, leaving their weapons and gear on the field.

Spottswood's unit fills in the trench area next to Broy's Georgians. Chambers nudges Spottswood and points out the gruesome scene beside them.

"Ain't those the crackers from camp back in Alabama?"

Spottswood looks straight ahead as he offers a reply. "Those are American soldiers returning from battle."

"They sure look like—"

Spottswood lifts the side of his helmet and cocks an ear toward the battlefield. "Shut up and listen."

Spottswood slides toward the rim of the trench, straining to hear something in the distance. Unable to define what he's hearing, he cautiously removes his helmet and listens intently. After several slow seconds, his eyes train on what his ears have detected.

A lone American, wounded, is hung up on barbed wire. Panicked, dazed, he is screaming for help. He has lost his helmet and gun and moves his hands and feet absently like a puppet with tangled strings. In the background, German soldiers talk in loud whispers.

"Help me! For the love of God, help me!" The lone American's cries increase in volume and terror with each passing moment.

Spottswood slides back from the trench's rim. He replaces his helmet with great purpose, firmly and deliberately tightening the chin strap like an athlete adjusting his equipment. Looking to his side, Spottswood sees Captain Broy wearing a disbelieving look.

"Captain Broy, sir, one of your men is trapped on the barbed wire about thirty yards out."

"Anybody out there is dead."

"Sir, he's calling to us. We can't just leave him."

"The Germans are using him as bait. They know inexperienced troops are sentimental. As soon as we go out to get him, they'll cut him, and us, to ribbons."

"I could get him."

Chambers gently grabs Spottswood by the elbow from behind. "Sarge, don't go crazy on us."

Broy walks over and grabs Spottswood by the collar of his coat. The lone American's screams grow louder and more desperate in the background.

"You dumb nigger, they are baiting us! If you go out there, I'll kill you before the Germans can. Don't even dream your friend Major Fish can get you out of the kind of trouble that comes with this degree of insubordination."

Spottswood considers Broy for a moment, then pushes him away with all his might, sending Broy sprawling. Spottswood grabs his rifle, fixes his bayonet, and releases the weapon's safety.

"Damn coward! That man trusted you with his life!" Spottswood says.

Before anyone can restrain him, he jumps over the rim of the trench and onto the battlefield.

Spottswood half crawls, half sprints across no-man's-land, stumbling over the dead and dying. At random intervals, wounded men grab and clutch vainly at Spottswood's uniform as he races by. In the background, the lone American's screams increase with shouts from the Germans. A few seconds later, bullets start streaking by Spottswood. The ground seems to explode, and the wooden posts holding up the barbed wire splinter.

Finding cover where he can, Spottswood returns fire. What follows is like a mad arcade game, with Germans popping up and down as Spottswood fires at them and reloads. Some Germans clutch their bodies as they are hit, others duck for cover.

Spottswood uses all his athletic skills, timing his movements so that he hits the ground and pops up between shots. When a German soldier jumps out from a trench directly in front of him, Spottswood clubs him with the butt of his rifle, then bayonets him.

In the trenches, Major Fish rushes to the sound of fire near his troops. Some of the American troops are cheering, some simply looking on in shock. Major Fish grabs Chambers, who is cheering as if he is at a ball game.

"What's going on?"

"Sergeant Poles went out to rescue one of those Georgia boys, sir."

"Don't stand there with your finger up your ass, give him covering fire."

Major Fish pulls his pistol from his holster, releases its safety and blows the whistle around his neck, signaling an attack. He pops over the rim of the trench, pistol blazing. His troops follow, laying down a murderous fire.

Spottswood, now in the middle of a firefight, struggles forward. Bullets whiz all around him. At last he crawls up to the lone American and starts cutting him loose from the barbed wire with a pair of wire cutters.

"Thank God, thank God!" The man makes Spottswood's work harder by grasping at him.

Just as Spottswood's fellow soldiers fight their way to his

position, a burst of machine gun fire cuts the lone American to pieces. His lifeless form falls in front of Spottswood.

Disbelieving, Spottswood gathers the shattered man's form in his arms, almost willing him to live. The lone American looks at him with a supreme look of gratitude, which turns to silent disbelief and despair as he dies.

Major Fish grabs Spottswood forcefully by the shoulder, pulling him back toward the American lines.

Chapter Twenty-Six

COURT-MARTIALED

EARLY THE NEXT MORNING, Spottswood is called to company head-quarters. The headquarters is but a hole in the wall of a large trench. It has a wood floor and a small table and chair, which Major Fish sits on.

Spottswood comes in and salutes.

Fish hesitantly returns the salute, a foreshadowing of the words that follow. "Sergeant Poles, despite your conspicuous act of bravery, Captain Broy has seen fit to bring you up on charges of insubordination."

"Sir, that man would have—"

"He died anyway, sergeant."

"Sir."

"What you did was brave, but that man was dead from the moment he was snagged on the wire. The Germans were using him as bait."

"I couldn't leave him."

"That's exactly what Captain Broy will say. He'll say colored troops are too emotional to follow orders in combat."

"Will I be tried by the French?"

"In matters of military justice, you are once again American. I will be your advocate, and Captain Broy will serve as prosecutor."

"What will you say in my defense?"

"I'll say you're the best damned man in my unit."

"Will that be enough?"

"I don't know. But the officer conducting the inquiry, Colonel Patton, should be of help to us. He's been known to fly off the handle himself. There's a rumor he killed a man with a trench shovel because he was displaying cowardice in the face of the enemy. He's possibly insane, which means you may have found a jury of your peers."

A long day of legal preparation leads to an early morning trip to division headquarters—an abandoned farmhouse. The only sign that it is an official hearing is a new American flag posted in one corner and a picture of President Wilson hanging on the wall. Light streaks in through broken windows and holes in the structure. Colonel George S. Patton Jr. sits behind a broken desk with an old book propping up one leg. Patton is a muscular man with close-cropped hair. His uniform is immaculate, right down to the sheen of his riding boots.

Patton carefully dusts the desk before setting out papers from a thin file. He is going over Captain Broy's written report. Broy, Fish, and Spottswood stand before him. There is a large figure in an officer's uniform in the shadows behind them.

"Captain Broy, why were your troops back in their trenches instead of attempting to take the enemy position as ordered?" Patton's voice is accusatory, which surprises Spottswood and Fish.

"Ran into heavy fire, sir."

"Heavy fire?"

"Yes, sir, heavy fire." A trace of nervousness leaks into Broy's voice, its pitch growing higher.

"There are varying degrees of 'heavy fire.' Had you ever been under fire before?"

"No, sir."

"The French officers supervising the 369th characterized the enemy's fire as 'moderate' and said you had a numerical superiority."

Broy's reply tumbles out, a bit of panic replacing the nervousness. "The French are jaded and think nothing of sacrificing vast numbers of troops for limited objectives. It was very heavy fire."

Patton examines a paper while considering this remark, then another. He puts down the paper and looks Broy straight in the eye.

"When you run from 'heavy' fire, is it your custom to leave your wounded on the field?"

"We had no choice, sir."

"You had a choice, captain. You could do what Sergeant Poles did, or you could have shot the poor dumb bastard so the Hun couldn't torture him."

"Shoot my own man?"

"It's better than leaving him as you did. I understand your unit and Major Fish's had an altercation back at camp in Alabama."

"Sir, that had no bearing—"

"Didn't it? Don't tell me you held no lingering resentment toward Major Fish and his unit."

"Sir, with all respect, the only reason we are here is because Sergeant Poles violated a direct order."

"So he did. And you're the kind of wet-faced weasel who will run all the way to General Pershing with an appeal if I don't see it your way."

"Sir?"

"It's a yes-sir, no-sir answer."

"Yes, sir."

"Yes, sir, you understand the question, or yes, sir, you're a wet-faced weasel?"

Broy looks stunned for a moment as he tries to compose himself. "Both sir."

"At least you're an honest weasel. What I need here is an unbiased observer who can tell me of Sergeant Poles' actions."

The figure from the back of the room moves from the shadows to the light by the side of the table. It is Christy Mathewson, the great New York Giants pitcher now a major in the American Expeditionary Force. Mathewson is movie-star handsome, a large, rugged, athletic man with wavy hair and an All-American face. Mathewson salutes Patton, and Patton returns it crisply.

Mathewson introduces himself formally to the court, as if any American male over the age of six didn't know who he is.

"Major Mathewson, sir. I can vouch for Sergeant Poles. I was with a group of French observers when Sergeant Poles executed his heroics. They were most impressed."

Patton laughs to himself for a moment. "Seems like nothing but a good whore or a bad bottle of wine impresses our hosts. That must have been a hell of thing you did out there sergeant. Captain Broy, do you have anything that might detract from the testimony of the great Christy Mathewson?"

"No, sir."

"Then get your yellow ass out of my sight and never let me hear of you leaving a man on the field again."

"Yes, sir."

Broy salutes and quickly leaves headquarters. The tension leaves the room with him, and Patton turns toward Spottswood. "At ease, sergeant. You should get a medal for what you did. Unfortunately, that would only rub salt in the wounds of an officer with political connections. I'm afraid you'll just have to do with the fact that I admire the hell out of you and that your own army will do you no harm."

"Thank you, sir."

Patton flicks casually through the papers on the desk before stopping and affixing his gaze on one. "I see from your papers that you are from Winchester, Virginia. I once had quite an adventure there."

"I remember it well, sir. I also remember seeing your grandfather."

"My grandfather?"

"Briefly, sir."

Patton considers this remark for a moment, then salutes Spottswood before going back to the papers before him. "I see. Dismissed, sergeant."

Spottswood and Major Fish salute, do an about-face in military fashion, and march out of the room.

Mathewson is waiting for Spottswood near the road. Spottswood offers Mathewson a salute, and Mathewson offers his hand. Spottswood takes his right hand from the brim of his hat and tentatively shakes.

"Christy Mathewson. I've been a fan for a long time."

Spottswood looks a bit sheepish. "First off, everybody knows who you are. Second, you don't have to flatter me by pretending you know who I am."

"We shared a stadium."

Mathewson turns away for a second and lets out several hacking coughs. He then takes a moment to compose himself before going on. Spottswood starts to offer an expression of concern, but Mathewson waves him off.

"It seemed like we were worlds apart." Spottswood decides to carry on the conversation.

"You were supposed to pretend my league didn't exist, and I was supposed to pretend I didn't know how much talent was in the Negro leagues."

"Look where pretending got us."

"Same place."

"Same place."

"It will happen again after the war."

"Supposing I don't do anything else stupid and get myself killed by the Germans or my own officers, how?"

"John McGraw has noticed you."

"What did he notice?"

"Noticed you covered center at the Polo Grounds, all 505 feet of it, better than anyone he'd ever seen."

"So he wants me as a defensive replacement?"

"Not after the way you hit the Tigers down in Havana in '16. He asked me to keep an eye on you."

"Is he ready to take on the fight it will take to get a colored man on a major league field?"

"McGraw? Born to fight."

"What about when the fact I was almost court-martialed, comes out?"

"When he hears the particulars, he'll only want you more."

"Sounds like a lunatic."

"That's what it will take to get a colored man in the bigs."

"I believe you have a point."

After the conversation with Mathewson, Spottswood rejoins Fish for the walk back to their unit. As they come over a high spot in the road, they see two columns of troops stretched out before them. On one side of the road is Spottswood's unit, the 369th. On the other are the white Georgians.

Major Fish stops and motions Spottswood to go ahead. Spottswood walks between the two ranks of troops. As he passes, soldiers on each side of the road salute him one by one. When Spottswood reaches the end of the line, a lone Georgian steps forward and presents him with a patch from his unit and an American helmet. Spottswood takes these items and regards them for a moment, then turns around and salutes all of the troops behind him. He turns and walks into the distance alone as the troops on both sides of the road hold their ranks and watch.

THE WEEKS THAT FOLLOW find the 369th much in demand. The French use them to assault positions previously thought impregnable. The 369th's losses are heavy, but its reputation for gallantry grows. Spottswood learns the pain of burying friends and seeing them taken, wounded, to the point of becoming numb.

As October of 1918 begins, he notices that the German defense is less ferocious. There are rumors of an armistice or all-out German surrender. Spottswood cares only that fewer of his friends are dying and that the calls to the front come less frequently.

On a particularly fine fall afternoon, Spottswood is reading a book when a runner from another unit dashes up before him preceded by a good fifteen seconds by the sound of his feet pounding the boards that line the bottom of the trench. The runner is white and wears an American uniform bearing the insignia of the 3rd Virginia.

"Sergeant Poles?"

Spottswood rises and salutes. The runner returns the salute as he catches his breath.

"What's so urgent?"

"The 3rd Virginia, Major Conrad. We need you to come quickly."

Spottswood throws down his book and grabs his helmet.

An hour's journey brings him to a small village four miles up the line. The courier leads Spottswood to the doors of an ancient church. Spottswood walks into the church tentatively. He is greeted by Captain Mike Foreman of the 3rd Virginia. Foreman is a slight man wearing glasses.

Foreman obviously dreads what he says next. "Tom, Major Conrad, said we should find you if anything should happen."

"How?" Spottswood can think of saying nothing else.

"He talked so proudly of you playing baseball in New York. He told us all about what you did for that Georgia boy."

"How?"

"We were attacking a strong point about six miles from here. He insisted on going out front. He urged everyone on when the fire grew heavy. We made it through the worst of it. Tom, Major Conrad, went forward—it was growing dark—to assess the enemy's strength. Someone behind him lit a cigarette; that's what the sniper must have seen. His helmet was raised because of the binoculars. The bullet hit him the only place it could."

"Where is he?"

Foreman opens the door to a small chapel. Tom, his skin ashen, lies on the altar covered by an American flag. His face resembles the alabaster statues atop the tombs lining the chapel's walls. Foreman closes the door behind him, leaving Tom and Spottswood alone. Candles burn around the altar, and the light filtering through the chapel's stained glass give the scene and feeling of unreality, a waking nightmare from which Spottswood cannot awaken.

Spottswood pulls close to Tom's lifeless form and examines the fatal wound despite himself. It is a small black hole, cleared of any blood, a small blemish on a serene face. Spottswood pulls himself back so that he stands next to Tom with his arms spread on the altar along the body, guarding that which is beyond harm.

Spottswood looks at Tom for a long time, tears finally welling in his eyes. At length, he collapses at the side of the altar, sobbing.

When he emerges from the chapel, Spottswood has but one sentence for Foreman: "We have to get him home."

"That will be almost impossible now."

"We have to bury him so that he can be retrieved later."

Foreman turns to two sergeants who do not need an order to know what must be done.

The men of the 3rd Virginia set to work.

George Washington Kurtz III, grandson of the man who grabbed Spottswood in Stonewall Cemetery nearly twenty years before, works in the furniture store/funeral parlor his family operates in a huge yellow building at the corner of Boscawen and Cameron streets (the Kurtzs brag that the comfort of the living and the dead is their family business).

A caisson that held shells is converted into a coffin; Kurtz lines the interior with the cleanest lumber he can find, carefully nailing each piece tightly in place to protect Tom from the elements.

Papers identifying Tom are placed in a waterproof dispatch pouch and secured beneath his hands. Spottswood places a cloth beneath the pouch so that the oilskin doesn't stain Tom's uniform. He doesn't know why, but it seems important.

Tom is buried in a corner of the churchyard. His comrades line the grave with stones to form a makeshift tomb. As the work continues by lantern light, members of the 3rd Virginia stream by to offer their respects. Some weep; others softly curse fate; all are obviously moved deeply by Tom's death. Kurtz chisels Tom's name as best he can on a large stone placed at the head of the grave. The work ends just as a cold sunrise bathes the French landscape in a gray light that mirrors the joyless Virginians it illuminates.

His work at the church finished, Spottswood goes in search of the man he knows will make sure Tom's body makes it home.

Finding George Patton is not difficult. His profane tirades and willingness to cajole, humiliate, or beat a man he considers insufficiently enthusiastic about combat is legendary throughout the AEF.

Armed with a pass from Foreman, Spottswood finds Patton at a forward position, his position much more forward than that of his troops. The scene before Spottswood is bizarre, even by the standards of war. Patton and another officer stand on a hill about thirty yards forward of the line, looking through binoculars, pointing in the distance, and exposing themselves to fire. Shells kick up dirt around them, and stray bullets whizz by at intervals close enough to have the troops behind them hunkered down in their trenches.

Under the guise of having an important message for Patton, Spottswood crawls up to the major who serves as Patton's aide de camp.

"Important message?" The major seems incredulous. "Nothing is more important now than the colonel showing General MacArthur he is the braver of the two."

"This message is vital."

"I'm sure as hell not going out there. If you care to risk your life on account of those two egotistical buffoons, be my guest."

Having survived one dramatic foray into no-man's-land, Spottswood thinks better of leaving the safety of the trenches. At length, the two officers return to the trenches, MacArthur departing in a staff car, leaving a fuming Patton in his wake.

"Son of a bitch questioned my ability to properly assess the enemy's position. Goddamn him!" Patton is railing at everyone and no one in particular.

The major holds Spottswood back until the tirade is complete.

"No demerits at the Academy! Perfect soldier! Mother lived off campus holding his goddamned hand the whole time! Father was a general, on the winning side of the War between the States, as if that makes a damn bit of difference now!"

Patton's face eventually turns a shade of color not associated with rage, and he notices Spottswood before him.

"Sergeant Poles, what brings you to my presence again?"

Spottswood holds forth an envelope containing the particulars of Tom's death and burial. "I have need of a military accommodation once offered to you."

Realizing the gravity of the situation, Patton gently takes the envelope from Spottswood's hands and carefully reads its contents. The message digested, Patton places the papers back in the envelope and secures them in the interior breast pocket of his field jacket.

"I will see to this."

George Patton keeps his word.

Chapter Twenty-Eight

FINAL ACTION AND HOMECOMING

THE WAR ENDED A FEW WEEKS LATER.

The 369th is involved in one more action, though it is not recorded among the Great War's mighty battles or anywhere but the hearts and minds of those who took part. But it is seared in the memory of the men who fought it—if *fought* is the proper word—for the rest of their life.

A cool early November morning found the 369th in a row of trenches guarding a road at the edge of the front lines, obscured by a heavy fog. The unrhythmic clinking of canteens and mess kits banging softly together amidst the sounds of horses' hooves and feet moving en masse comes from the direction of the road.

Major Fish climbs to the rim of the trench and trains binoculars on the area from which the sounds are coming. After a moment, he motions Spottswood to his side and hands him the field glasses.

Straining to see through the mist, Spottswood finally makes out a column of Germans marching in unmilitary fashion—no defined ranks, rifles held haphazardly. Some look like boys, others the sick and walking wounded usually left in the rear echelon. Horses pull several wagons randomly packed with men using food sacks as pillows as they try to find a rhythm in which they can sleep.

Spottswood hands the binoculars back to Fish.

"Their war is over."

"We can't chance that. The morning fog will burn off soon. They could spot us and decide to rejoin the hostilities."

Fish summons the runners who are always near him to spread orders to the rest of the unit.

"Pass the word: rifles ready to fire in two minutes. Stay down until you hear my signal, then open fire on the field directly in front of us. Two volleys from the trenches, then advance firing. Tell the men to stay no more than three feet apart. I don't want men getting lost in the fog and taking friendly fire."

The runners sprint off noiselessly. Spottswood loads his rifle and clicks off the safety. His hands play along the weapon's stock as they once did along the handle of a bat. After what seems like an hour, Fish puts whistle to mouth. After a shrill blast, the 369th pops up from its trenches firing. Orange flashes of light pierce the fog up and down the line.

Spottswood fires twice, not sure what he is aiming at, then leaves the trench and begins advancing across the field. At his sides, men fire and reload as they cover yards of ground that, just a few months before, were measured in hundreds of lives.

The fog holds the smoke discharged from the rifles, and the area reeks of sulfur, men choking on the thick air as they advance. Before them is screaming and shouting as the stunned Germans fall to the ground and try to organize a counterattack. The fire from the enemy is sporadic and ineffective. As soon as a German's location is revealed by the flash from his muzzle, several members of the 369th fire on his now-exposed position.

Spottswood lets four rounds go before he and his comrades find themselves in the chaotic ranks of the enemy. Men and horses writhe, wounded, on the ground. Wounded who show signs of resistance are shot at close range or clubbed (bayonets had not been fixed in order to preserve the accuracy of the rifles).

After a few moments, a German officer shouts in English, "Don't shoot! We surrender!" His plea is soon picked up with varying degrees of fluency by his troops.

Fish lets go a blast on his whistle followed "Cease fire!" Sporadic pops of gunfire chase his words. "Cease fire, damn you!"

Silence.

The American commander looks about him and gives out an order that seems reverse in priority: "Shoot suffering animals and treat the wounded."

To emphasize this order, Fish puts his Smith & Wesson .45 to the head of a badly wounded mare and pulls the trigger. The heavy thud of the animal hitting the ground is followed by similar sounds up and down the line.

"Sergeant Poles, take a squad and search the wagons for wounded and stragglers."

Spottswood points to five men around him and leads them into a cluster of wagons. Moving slowly and silently with his rifle before him in a firing position, he can see boots sticking out from the wheels of a wagon before him.

Spottswood moves quickly and noiselessly until he is standing over the boots' owner, the owner's head clearly in the middle of Spottswood's sites.

A boy, maybe seventeen or younger, looks up at Spottswood. His eyes burn bright blue—all the more so as his face turns ashen from loss of blood. Glancing down, Spottswood sees the boy is losing a fight to keep his intestines inside his uniform tunic.

"Bitte."

Spottswood feels his finger begin to squeeze the trigger. Is the boy asking for pity or release from the lingering death that awaits him?

"Bitte."

A split second before firing, Spottswood releases the pressure from the trigger and puts on the safety. He pulls the rifle back, ejects a bullet from the chamber, and lays it upon the ground before walking back into the morning mist.

He will never pick up a weapon in anger again.

The war effectively over less than two weeks later, the 369th goes back to being American, burying the countless dead and counting those who can't be identified before placing them in mass graves. Spottswood becomes numb to the carnage before him. Every face he sees, no matter how mangled or decayed, reminds him of Tom.

This terrible task is interrupted at times by the presentation of medals. The French, and belatedly the Americans, honor Spottswood for his bravery.

The war ends officially for the 369th when it boards a troop ship in Le Havre, beginning the crossing to New York.

The voyage home is uneventful.

The ship, having carried thousands of troops home before the 369th, stinks. Men play cards, drink, and attempt to sleep as the vessel heaves and pitches. Spottswood doesn't take part in the games, though he's always invited, and seems troubled and aloof to his fellow soldiers.

Spottswood writes Emma at every opportunity, but there has been no reply. He knows her stubborn pride will not allow her to express concern for his foolish venture because like all wars, the journey he embarked on is foolish.

It is a cold February day in 1919 when Spottswood's ship docks in New York. There are no bands or grand parades to greet the 369th. Major Fish says his farewell to the troops the night before and vanishes into the winter chill as soon as the ship docks. Looking about at the docks and the joyous reunions around him, Spottswood quietly shoulders his duffel bag, says a few heartfelt goodbyes, then begins trudging toward home.

Spottswood's pace, for once, is slow. After months of dread, he doesn't want his worst suspicions confirmed.

As the apartment door opens, Emma is cleaning house. Spottswood doesn't know if he should be relieved or tensed for a battle yet to come. She goes about her business as he waits for a big welcome.

Spottswood drops his duffel bag and holds his cap in his hands before him. "A lot of families came to the docks to greet us."

"Go back to the docks, and see if you can find one that will have you."

"Is that any way to greet your husband?"

"Husband? I have a man who's on the road playing ball half the time. When he gets old enough to quit, he runs off to fight the war."

"Life must be hard for you."

"Must be. Why should I take you back?"

"Because I took your heart and never gave it back."

"How do you know you took my heart?"

"Because you took mine."

"Is that so?"

"Every time I look in the mirror, I see the look of a person whose heart rests in the hands of another. I see that same look when I see you."

"How do you know it's you who has my heart?"

"The same way I knew we were meant for each other the second our eyes met."

"I think you've been reading some dirty French novels."

"At least I can read."

"How do they turn out?"

"Not with the hero watching his wife clean when he returns from war."

"That's how this one ends."

Emma grabs a feather duster and begins furiously dusting the glass globe on a lamp.

"If that's the case, I have something to return to you."

Spottswood reaches into his pocket and pulls out the card Emma gave him many years before and places it on the table before Emma. Emma looks at the card for a moment as tears begin to form in her eyes.

Spottswood lunges at Emma, who tries to get away. He catches her and gathers her in his arms. After putting up a half-hearted struggle for a moment, she begins kissing him passionately.

That night, Spottswood and Emma lie in bed talking with just the pale moonlight illuminating them.

"My world has changed so much," Spottswood clutches Emma's hand as these words come forth.

"You've seen so much."

"It's what I didn't see."

"What didn't you see?"

"I didn't see Tom in France, not while he was alive. We were only a few miles apart."

"That wasn't your fault."

"I couldn't be there when Major Conrad died. They say the Spanish influenza killed him, but I know it was Tom's death. Tom was his pride."

"Major Conrad was always proud of you."

"No. Tom was his pride. I was his guilt and shame."

"You have nothing to be guilty for or ashamed of."

"I feel as though I have never really had a family."

"You have me," Emma rolls over and softly kisses Spottswood. "That is, you have me unless you run off and do something stupid again."

"There's a way I can stay closer to you."

"Quit baseball and work at the haberdashery?"

"Play for the Giants."

"You already play for the Giants."

"Not the Elite Giants, the New York Giants."

"How many times, exactly, were you struck in the head in France?"

"Over in France, I ran into Christy Mathewson. He said John McGraw wanted to give me a chance."

"Men talk malarkey under stress."

"I proved myself on the battlefield. Now I'll prove myself in the major leagues."

"I don't want to see your heart broken."

"That would only happen if I lost you."

Spottswood pulls Emma close to him and kisses her on the forehead as his eyes close.

Chapter Twenty-Nine

McGRAW

THE 1919 SEASON BEGINS IN LATE APRIL, and Spottswood falls into the routines that have defined his adult life.

Despite Mathewson's promise that John McGraw, the New York Giants, and fame would find him, the season passes as it always has. Spottswood quickly regains his form and is once again the biggest baseball star outside the white world. His winter passes in expectation of a new season and dread that the call to the major leagues will never come.

A spring afternoon in 1920 finds him taking fielding practice at the Polo Grounds. John McGraw walks up behind him.

McGraw is a squat, fleshy man whose acerbic nature cuts through the flabbiness of his skin. McGraw squirms a bit in his formal suit; it's obvious this is not his preferred mode of dress. He tugs at the starched collar time and again.

A coach hits balls off the wall, and Spottswood measures the bounces as they come off the wood of varying consistency.

"Testing the tension of the wall?" McGraw's tone is flat, as one talking shop to someone with whom he is familiar.

"They replaced two sections; two others are rotted." Spottswood doesn't turn as he speaks.

"Matty said you were meticulous."

A ball hits the wall, and Spottswood fields it.

"How is Christy?"

"Poor bastard took the tuberculosis from getting gassed. I'm afraid he's not long for us."

Another ball hits the wall, and Spottswood fields it. "No matter how many times I've seen death, I still never accept it."

"Before we forget the war, Matty told me what you did, trying to save that poor bastard on the barbed wire."

"Had to do it."

"That's the kind of man I want on my team, has to be brave, can't help it."

"That kind of foolish bravery will let me play with whites?"

A ball hits the wall. Spottswood fields it and holds it, turning toward McGraw. McGraw takes his cue. "Baseball needs help in a big way. Series was fixed last year; everybody knows that. Popularity is low. Bring coloreds into the stands, and you might save the game."

"So you want me to play for the good of the game?"

"Hell no! I want you to play for the good of John McGraw and the New York Giants. I was nine games off the Reds last year, and they were no damn good. With you leadin' off and playing center between Pep Young and George Burns, I could win the pennant by ten games."

"You're a great philosopher."

"I'm a great baseball man. Philosophy has nothin' to do with it, just winnin'."

"I can help you win."

"Know you can. How old are you?"

"Old as I need to be."

"Still hit and run like before the war?"

"I can hit anywhere, anytime. I'll grab a bat right now if you want. Running is timing, knowing when to run. I know when to run."

"Save that for when it counts. What counts now is that we get you to Judge Landis and get him to give you the okay to join us."

"People say Judge Landis is a very tough man."

"That's what he'd have you think. Railroads had him in their pocket when he was on the bench. Racist bastard, too. I can make him see things my way."

Spottswood flips the ball to the coach and motions for him to hit again.

"I've heard some talk of your arm losing something."

Spottswood yells toward the infield. "Coming in!" Spottswood fields the ball off the wall, turns, and fires a rope to the third baseman.

McGraw admires the throw.

"Mr. Poles, prepare to make history."

"You're sure America is ready for a Negro in the major leagues?"

"I have been pushing them toward that idea. In 1913, I signed Jim Thorpe. Played off and on for me through '17. Kept him off the sauce, but I couldn't keep him away from football. That's the game he loves. Chose the Canton Bulldogs over New York. Can you beat that? He hit .252 for me, and people loved him. You hit .350 for me, win a pennant, and they'll put a statue in your honor in the middle of Broadway."

Chapter Thirty

KENESAW MOUNTAIN LANDIS

THE OFFICE OF BASEBALL'S COMMISSIONER is a legalistic affair, with books and briefs stacked all about. The walls are covered with dark oak paneling. The darkness is deepened by heavy green drapes and blinds covering the windows.

What little light there is comes from small brass lamps with green glass shades. Its occupant, Kenesaw Mountain Landis, dressed in a black suit with a white shirt and black tie, sits behind a massive oak desk, which dwarfs him.

The dominant feature on Landis's head is a huge shock of white hair, which plays off a set of dark eyes. Landis's eyes dart about the room as he talks, giving the impression that he's speaking to someone other than the person in front of him.

Spottswood and McGraw, dressed in the finest suits Dixon's Haberdashery can offer, sit in front of Landis in uncomfortable, low-backed chairs. The effect is of mortals speaking to the gods on Olympus. Landis speaks with the low, measured tone of a jurist, which makes even the most banal pronouncement seem learned.

He closes the file on a thick sheaf of papers before him.

"Mr. McGraw, I must say your case for Mr. Poles is well thought out."

"Thank you, Mr. Commissioner."

"Nonetheless, I am afraid baseball is not yet ready for colored players."

McGraw's temper, barely below the surface in the quietest of times, explodes. "Baseball, or the thieving sons of bitches you represent?"

"I'm going to ignore that, Mr. McGraw."

"Ignore me all you want, judge, but let this man ply his trade where God intended him to."

"In addition to the interest of the Giants, I am thinking in terms of the owners of the Negro Leagues, several of whom are quite distressed. They are afraid their business will be ruined if their best players are allowed into the majors."

"More sons of bitches! They outlawed slavery almost sixty years ago, yet they still treat their players as slaves."

"I'm well aware of history and slavery, Mr. McGraw. My father fought against it. I bear the name of a battle in which he suffered wounds he bore the rest of his days."

"And I'll bet he's damn proud of you now."

"That's enough!" For the first time, Landis's voice rises above the decibel level of the bench. He rises from his chair to make his presence more imposing.

McGraw is not impressed by this departure from decorum and raises his voice even more. "You let gamblers like Cobb and Tris Speaker remain in the game; everybody knows they're in on fixes! But you won't let a colored man play!"

"Speaking of gambling, there's the games Mr. Poles played in

Cuba some years ago."

"Of which Cobb was also a part!"

"Mr. McGraw, I think you fail to see the bigger picture here." Landis resumes his judicial demeanor.

"I see it just fine, and a sorry sight it is!"

"You would rip the fabric of society apart so the Giants could win."

"I'd march into hell itself if they had some ballplayers who would help the New York Giants win."

Landis rises and motions toward the door. "Good day, Mr. McGraw."

Landis resumes his seat and begins reviewing a file on his desk. His shaking hands bear witness that business has not returned to normal.

McGraw waits for a second before delivering his parting words. "It will not be a good day while we're breathing the same air."

"Good day, Mr. McGraw."

McGraw storms out of the room, slamming a massive oak door behind him. Spottswood waits silently for a moment, then quietly follows. Landis makes no eye contact as he leaves.

The cool of the evening does little to cool McGraw's temper. McGraw and Spottswood walk down the street together and stop under the light of a single lamp. McGraw offers Spottswood a drink from a flask, which Spottswood declines.

"If you don't start drinking after this, you never will. Why didn't you put up a fight in there?"

"Couldn't get in a word edgewise."

"I have a tendency to get agitated."

"That's a luxury a colored man can't afford."

"And a pity that is. A greater pity that I never had you play for my team."

McGraw sticks out his hand, Spottswood shakes it. They part in the night.

Chapter Thirty-One

THE HOUSE ON WATER STREET

TOM NEVER MARRIED.

After Major Conrad's death, the house on Water Street becomes Adelaide Conrad's by default. The girlish youth who charmed Winchester in 1878 has settled into an uncertain late middle age. No longer a beauty, she is past the age to attract fashionable suitors. Lacking money, she is no longer welcome by the new generation of wealthy in New York and Newport.

Adelaide comes back to the Lavender Room with trunks of outdated dresses and no head for business. The Conrad affairs, most recently handled by Tom, fall out of order, and tradesmen begin to avoid what had once been Winchester's most prominent home.

Conrad House's growing state of disrepair is magnified by a glowing new neighbor across the street.

The Market House, once the hub of local commerce, is demolished to make way for a new city hall. Not to be outdone by the carpet-bagging Judge Handley, native son Charles Broadway Rouss pays thirty thousand dollars—roughly half the building's cost—to ensure his name is etched over the door. Rouss begins his fabled business career selling pins and needles at the Market House before making a fortune selling dry goods in New York City.

Construction on Rouss City Hall begins in May 1900, and the grand edifice is opened to the public in March 1901. Rouss lives to see the building completed, but never actually "sees" it, having gone blind several years before construction began.

In uncharitable moments, Major Conrad says the building must have been designed by a blind man. Richardsonian Romanesque, Classical, English Gothic, and Victorian features are all evident in city hall's exterior, sometimes clashing violently as each tries to assert its dominance in an architectural theme that is never really evident. The interior reflects the exterior's eclectic nature. There are rooms for the Winchester City Council, of which Tom was a member, circuit court, the treasurer's office, the Hiram Masonic Lodge, and on its top floor, the building's crown jewel, a 770-seat theater. (Mary Pickford and John Philip Sousa are among the notables to grace its stage.)

The walls and ceilings of the theater are decorated by frescoes of Italian design. During shows, magic lanterns project clouds that appear to move across the vaulted ceiling. The effect is of watching entertainment in a celestial realm.

Although not a beneficiary of the Handley fortune, Adelaide makes sure her kinsman is not forgotten when it comes to con-structing grand buildings to meet the needs of Winchester's growing populace. In 1913, she dedicates the Handley Library, a Beaux-Arts vision at the corner of Braddock and Piccadilly streets. The build-ing is shaped like a book with the rotunda at its front serving as the spine and two wings shooting out like the pages of an open book (something the locals of Winchester note that Adelaide has never been). In 1922, Adelaide helps lay the cornerstone at Handley High

School, which is next to the newly named Handley Boulevard on the south end of town. Its columned façade, rising from a small hill, give it a commanding presence no other building in the Shenandoah Valley can match.

Adelaide's increasingly rare social appearances are matters of laughter for the town's upper crust and those who aspire to be. Her dress is always a decade or two—perhaps three—out of style with hoops and flowing bodices and hats that feature an aviary's worth of feathers. Adelaide's proud bearing is undercut by the fact that the whole town knows of her near-poverty.

Aside from acts of civil largesse, Adelaide is rarely seen outside the house on Water Street. The exiled Pennsylvanians, who now dominate not only Washington but Stewart Street in their grand houses, cannot forgive the fact that she abandoned them for a grander level of society years before. The invitations to visit Conrad House are rarely accepted and, after a few years, not offered.

Lucy is the only other person living in the grand house on Water Street, and it is clearly beyond her ability to maintain.

During the winter of 1922, Spottswood makes his first visit in years to Winchester.

He has written faithfully to Lucy without reply. This doesn't particularly alarm him because of her illiteracy and stubborn nature.

Spottswood phones once a week on Sunday afternoons when he is home in New York. The conversations are short and never of any true substance. There is always a feeling of someone else listening. This is amplified by the distant click that is always heard shortly after Lucy picks up the phone.

Lucy makes it plain that she does not wish to visit New York, let alone live there. Spottswood will have to visit her. Arrangements are made.

It is made clear before Spottswood's visit that he and Emma will not be staying at Conrad House. Spottswood arranges for a room in a private house on North Kent Street. He climbs the limestone stairs to his former home a stranger.

Upon entering the front door, Spottswood notices the shudder from Emma beside him. Large chunks of wallpaper give up their tenuous hold on the wall and peel in sheets from the top. Cobwebs are clearly visible in almost every corner. The eternal fire in Major Conrad's study is out, and the small enclosure is cold as a tomb.

The most disturbing thing Spottswood discovers are piles of his unopened letters sitting on a counter in the pantry; Adelaide refuses to read them to Lucy. In a moment of what she believes is compassion, Emma wonders aloud why Lucy didn't ask one of her fellow parishioners to read the letters to her. "So I can hear how you've made the son I raised better than I could have?" is Lucy's icy response. This brief observation sets the tone for the interaction between mother and daughter-in-law for years to come.

Icy describes the general atmosphere in the house on Water Street.

Adelaide takes her meals, and virtually lives, in the Lavender Room. Lucy lives on the third floor and eats in the kitchen. The dining room is set every day, broken down at night, and re-set the next morning.

Spottswood extends his stay in 1922 to do what repairs he can. He will be a more frequent visitor during the next two decades to do what work he can with Adelaide's permission. He is not allowed to stay in the house.

Adelaide dies from a late-night fall down the front staircase in 1943. She tumbles, tripping over an ancient velvet dressing gown that was the rage at the Vanderbilt's summer estate, Breakers, in

1892. Adelaide lies, moaning softly, on the cold foyer floor until dawn the next morning when Lucy finds her. A doctor is summoned, but he quickly determines nothing of substance can be done. Adelaide is carried gently to the Lavender room where she dies that afternoon, surrounded by images of the family she never really knew.

Lucy is evicted shortly thereafter by a very polite lawyer who assures her nothing can be done. She leaves the house in which she has lived for nearly eighty years with little more than a suitcase and a wealth of memories she would do best to forget.

In 1947, it's decided Rouss City Hall needs parking for bureaucrats, those they serve, judges, those they judge, and the dwindling number of theatergoers who wish Mary Pickford was still on the stage. Conrad House, where George Washington and Robert E. Lee slept and generations of Conrads generated success and secrets, is torn down. All that is left of it is the native limestone retaining wall that protected the house from rising tides of all kinds at its front, the staircase, and the iron hitching post where Lee tied Traveler.

Winchester's City Council accomplishes in short order what Sheridan's Federals failed to do on a warm September afternoon in 1864.

Concerned citizens try to save the home as a historic landmark worthy of restoration. They are too small in number to defeat progress. Out of their efforts, Preservation of Historic Winchester, a group that will bedevil developers and those who espouse modern architecture for decades, is born, but too late to preserve its greatest jewel.

Before the house is leveled, an auction of its contents is held to settle Adelaide's debts. African Americans, even those who once lived there, are not allowed to bid. In death, white Winchester puts a protective wall around the Conrads. None of their belongings will end up in an African American home. Better the garbage than that.

Major Conrad's Confederate uniforms, dress and field, are bought by the historical society, packed neatly into boxes, promptly stored and forgotten. (Major Conrad insisted he be buried in civilian clothes.) His law books soon grace the shelves of lesser colleagues in offices around the courthouse square.

Adelaide's dresses are bought in bulk and are soon a staple at little girls' tea parties. Fashionable visions that once graced the halls of the Whitneys and Vanderbilts are seen in Winchester's backyards and treehouses for more than a decade to come.

Chapter Thirty-Two

THE NEW BREED

SPOTTSWOOD HARDLY RECOGNIZES BASEBALL as it moves into the middle of the 1920s. The home run becomes coin of the realm. Tactical baseball gives way to Herculean drives leaving the playing field. Spottswood finds himself agreeing with Ty Cobb about the strategic nature of the game vanishing as crowds, and an increasing number of managers, wait for the long ball to carry them to victory.

The catalyst for this change is literally in Spottswood's house.

Babe Ruth comes to the Yankees in a deal for the cash Red Sox owner Harry Frazee needs to put on a Broadway play (at least it's a hit: *No, No, Nanette*). Ruth hits fifty-four home runs (as few as eight have led the American League in previous seasons) in 1920 and fifty-nine the following year.

The Yankees share the Polo Grounds with the Giants and Elite Giants starting in 1913. In 1921, the Yankees draw 350,000 more fans than the Giants to their home field. McGraw has had enough. "The Yankees will have to build a park in Queens or some other out-of-the-way place and wither on the vine," McGraw tells his owners, who promptly evict the Yankees.

The Yankees chose to "wither" just across the Harlem River. In a year, Yankee Stadium rises on ten acres in the Bronx only a mile from the Polo Grounds. Looking down upon it from Coogan's bluff, Spottswood sees the future.

He is not part of it.

Speed is no longer treasured by managers and owners. Once Spottswood's greatest commodity, it has begun to decline. Spottswood wonders if he left too much of his prime on the fields of France, while denying the obvious: he's growing older. An upstart, James "Cool Papa," Bell of the St. Louis Stars, soon becomes the chief topic of conversation in discussions of the fastest center fielder in the Negro Leagues. Knowing every trick in the book, Spottswood camouflages his weaknesses. Without saying a word, Walker also makes concessions in this department with unscheduled days off.

While Spottswood's wounded psyche says "no" to such offers, his aching body almost always says "yes."

With a short right field in Yankee Stadium tailored to his swing, Ruth is soon obliterating every offensive record in his path. His appeal stretches deep into the African American community. There is a whispering campaign, accepted as truth by many, that Ruth is partly African American. He becomes a surrogate for those who wish to see an African American whose heritage is not whispered about on a major-league field.

Ruth's off-the-field antics—womanizing, drinking, and general merry-making—are on a scale with his on-field heroics. Players are growing more brash, another thing the self-effacing Spottswood can't stand.

This trend extends to the Negro Leagues.

Spottswood and two teammates, Hubert Jackson and Stan

Morgan, sit on the ground stretching before a game in August 1929 when the brashest of all Negro League players strolls toward them wearing the road uniform of the Birmingham Black Barons.

"Here it comes," Morgan mutters under his breath.

Satchel Paige nonchalantly greets his three rivals. Paige is tall and thin with a carefully cropped mustache. His uniform looks tailored, and his air is arrogant.

"E-lite Giants! Old men and children."

"Take it somewhere else." Spottswood speaks with an authoritative voice, the clarion of doom to a younger player in his day.

Paige doesn't flinch.

"Just being social." Paige throws open his arms in mock indignity.

"This is not a social event."

"We're all friends." Paige persists.

"No friends within these walls."

Paige's amicability disappears. "Grandpa, you'd better hope I'm friendly to you. I take pity on the elderly."

Spottswood stands up and places himself in Paige's face. "I need the pity of no man, especially a braying jackass who's trying to strike me out with his mouth."

Paige glares at Spottswood and walks away.

The rage Paige's impertinence sparks in Spottswood causes the older man's mind to drift. In the on-deck circle before his first at-bat, there is a distinct image in Spottswood's mind that blocks out the game before him. A row of African American troops stand in a trench. Only their heads are visible at ground level. An artillery barrage is going on in no-man's-land before them. The reflection of the explosions shines off their helmets.

There is the crack of a bat.

Spottswood snaps out of his reverie. The batter before him has singled. He shakes his head and strides to the plate. Paige is on the mound.

"Look who's shufflin' up to the plate! Shouldn't you be back in Ole Virginy pickin' cotton, old man?"

Spottswood digs in. The first pitch is a ferocious fastball that Spottswood swings at late and misses.

"Sit down, grandpa. I'm just going to embarrass you."

Paige winds up quickly but throws a change-up. Spottswood lays off, and it's called a ball.

"At least you're not senile. Thinkin' you can hit me and hittin' me are two different things." Paige goes into an exaggerated wind-up, his lead leg reaching above his head. The lead leg comes down far in front of the pitching rubber and Paige's entire weight follows it, fueling an incredible fastball.

Spottswood times the pitch and slaps it into left field. Running with all his might, Spottswood makes second base, barely beating the throw.

"Lot closer than it used to be, Spotts!" Paige seems totally unperturbed that Spottswood has just driven in a run.

"Where I am standing? Shut up and pitch" is the reply.

The next batter bloops a single to left, almost too short for Spottswood to score. Spottswood, who is off at the crack of the bat, hits third in full stride and turns for home. A few feet past the bag, Spottswood's hamstring explodes, and he falls to the ground, writhing in pain. After a second, he raises himself to his knees and, using his one good leg, tries to crawl home.

Paige is standing forty feet down the line, waiting to cut off the throw from the outfield. "Spotts! Are you okay?"

Spottswood crawls forward, every movement more painful than the last. The throw comes in from the outfield, and Paige catches it reflexively, more concerned about Spottswood than the ball.

"Tag me!" The tone of Spottswood's voice is defiant but can't mask the pain behind his gritted teeth.

Paige begins walking up the line.

"Are you okay?"

"Tag me, damn you!"

Paige kneels down and, almost embarrassed, tags Spottswood. Paige grabs Spottswood under the arms and lifts him so that their faces are just inches apart.

"Never hesitate to tag a runner! Never cheat the game!"

Spottswood leaves the field with the help of his teammates and, once out of sight of the crowd, is carried to the locker room. Amber light seeps in from the high windows and casts a glow on the small space, the slow dripping from the showers in the next room the only noise.

Spottswood sits on a bench slowly taking off his uniform. He is the only player in the clubhouse. His teammates have returned to the game. Spottswood looks at each piece of his uniform as he removes it, carefully regarding it and turning it over in his hands before folding it neatly and placing it on the bench beside him.

Walker, still in uniform, comes up behind Spottswood. Walker is gray and stooped and seems to be carrying a heavy weight upon his back. He sits down on the bench next to Spottswood with Walker facing one way, Spottswood the other.

"One more season. You heal well."

"What's the point?"

"You're still the best I have."

"That's not enough anymore."

Walker hangs his head and speaks only after a long silence. "I thought it would be you."

"Me too" is the whispered response.

Walker places his hand upon Spottswood's shoulder as the men turn to look one another in the eye. "He's still out there. If you find him, or he finds you, help him."

Spottswood clasps Walker's hand. "At least I didn't wear a headdress."

Walker rises slowly and unsteadily, turns, and walks away to leave Spottswood with his thoughts. Spottswood picks up his cap and turns it over in his hands.

Walker dies shortly thereafter in his native Ohio. Reflecting years later, Spottswood decides it might be just as well his mentor didn't live to see the demise of the Negro Leagues.

The end of Spottswood's career is only the beginning of hard times for both him and the world in general.

The stock market crash leaves New York a shell of its once-prosperous self. There is no longer a calling for fine men's clothing, and Dixon's Haberdashery closes in 1931. Its proprietor dies shortly thereafter: a broken heart is as good a reason to put on the death certificate as any. The brownstone is sold but not nearly for its worth.

Faced with an uncertain future, Spottswood convinces Emma to return with him to Winchester. She dreads the manners and mores of the South but gives in to the reality that there is no longer a safe economic haven for her and Spottswood in New York.

Chapter Thirty-Three

BUILDING A BUSINESS

THE FIRST ORDER OF BUSINESS on Spottswood's return is locating a home. He finds one at 530 Fremont Street with enough room that Lucy can move in from the house on Water Street after her eviction. Lucy and Emma reach an uneasy truce, though Emma never gets used to the fine dining setting prepared before each night's meal.

The modest structure is in an area reserved for Winchester's freedmen since colonial times. Located on what was the outskirts of town, the area has long been a home to tradesmen, blacksmiths being the most enduring. Over time, Winchester grows around it. The African American section of town has streets with names like *Liberty* and *Lincoln,* the latter running along the wall of the National Cemetery, where Federal dead are buried.

Prosperity for people of color is tolerated as long as it stays within certain geographic and economic limits. Too much success is not tolerated. So it is that the six members of the Brown family who become doctors—among them a female, Fairfax—are forced to practice and teach in Washington and Pittsburgh. The only time they are welcomed back into the community is when they are buried in Orrick Cemetery, the African American cemetery along the Valley Pike.

When Conrad House is demolished, a sympathetic contractor allows Spottswood to haul away several truckloads of yellow bricks. With these, Spottswood constructs a gazebo at the back of his small lot where Lucy can be found most evenings, staring silently in the direction of her former home.

For a business opportunity, Emma finds a cab company at the corner of Kent and Piccadilly streets available for a song. The former owners had been none too industrious, and Emma calculates that all that is needed for success is a few reliable machines and a strong work ethic.

Livery businesses and then cabs have long been a staple of Winchester's African American community. A former slave and noted minister, Robert Orrick makes his mark in this field when he obtains a contract hauling mail during Reconstruction.

Using the money he saves from baseball, along with what is gained from the sale of the Dixon properties in New York, Spottswood sets out to become a prominent businessman and community leader. Despite his mechanical inclinations, Spottswood realizes that he will need someone with an intricate knowledge of automobiles to get his new business on firm footing.

He calls Will Slavin.

The years between Damon Runyon's great race of 1915 and 1932 are not kind to Will. A kerosene lamp at his petrol station bursts into flames and reigns liquid fire upon him, leaving a terrible red scarring on his face and upper body. The New York State Thruway Commission opens a deluxe turnpike between New York City and the more-friendly suburbs to the north. The Vanderbilts and Whitneys, what remains of them, need no longer make a stop in Sloatsburg.

Will rides the rails south, reaching Winchester in less than a week. Unlike other hobos, he carries a fine leather bag not unlike those clutched in doctors' hands, filled with mechanic's tools. There is more than one brawl in the hobo camps that dot the railway lines as Will defends, always successfully, the tools of his trade. Looking at the stock of reasonably priced vehicles available, he settles on three Model Ts with which to begin Spottswood's transportation empire. Although Ford stops making them in '28, the Model Ts have plenty of parts available, if only from local junkyards; are easy to maintain; and are light on gas. Working for a month with little rest, Will and Spottswood soon have the cars working and restored to a state if not of opulence, at least of respectability.

Will lives in the garage, as much to provide security as to respect the dictates of races living together, without the African Americans being servants, in the South. For years after his departure, children in the area of Kent and Piccadilly streets talk in hushed tones about the "monster" that once lived at the cab company.

Business being good, Spottswood's next acquisition after the Model Ts is a Lincoln hearse. People lying in the back of this ornate vehicle seem not to care about the ethnicity of the person at the wheel.

Next is a 1932 Packard DeLuxe Eight. Packard is advertised as the car for people who "knew the difference" and this vehicle is always in demand for weddings and funerals. Spottswood soon discovers that weddings and funerals are the two things for which appearances must be kept up; damn the price.

The Packard is flashy, fast, and loud.

Spottswood nicknames it "Satchel."

There is one person whom all the cab companies, white and African American, in Winchester are loathe to serve.

On a hot summer evening—June 25, 1906—Harry Kendall Thaw,

goes to the rooftop theater at Madison Square Garden. After several false starts, Thaw approaches the table of Stanford White, the Garden's architect, widely regarded as the greatest designer of buildings in America. As White listens to "I Could Love a Million Girls," Thaw takes a pistol from his coat and pumps three slugs into White's head.

Thaw obsesses over the architect because of a previous relationship between White and Thaw's wife, Evelyn Nesbit. Nesbit is a great beauty, whom White first spies when she is performing in *The Wild Rose*. (Nesbit is still in her mid-teens.) As revealed at Thaw's trial, White allegedly does some harrowing things to the future Mrs. Thaw, including drugging her to take her virginity; making her entertain him on a red velvet swing (the tales vary on her state of undress during this exercise, though "silk stockings" are always mentioned); and acts so unmentionable they have to be passed to the judge and jury on slips of discreetly folded paper.

Such slips are passed at two trials, which result in Thaw being sent to an asylum after being found "not guilty by reason of insanity" for White's death. He is judged sane and released in July 1915. Thaw's father, a "Pittsburgh coal baron," has to find a place to hide his wayward progeny. Someplace removed from polite society, but able to afford Thaw the lifestyle to which he is accustomed.

It is decided to call in an old social debt from Adelaide Conrad. Conferring with the refugees from the Johnstown Flood, it is decided that none of the grand homes on Washington and Stewart streets are suitable for Thaw. (Negligently allowing a dam to break is far less a crime than shooting a prominent citizen in the head.) An estate, Kenilworth, in Clearbrook, a discreet distance from town, is purchased at a bankruptcy sale. Once a prosperous farm, it is now a secluded sanctuary.

What goes on inside Kenilworth's stately limestone walls soon becomes the topic of much local conversation.

Thaw populates his home with a rotating group of exotic women, women with titles such as "countess" and "duchess." In the years following World War I, there are many such titles floating about, attached to people with much allure but little money. The ranks of these women never include a "princess." Thaw does not want to appear to be a social climber.

Intrigued by the titles of these women and the loose sexual habits associated with Thaw and European women in general, the upper echelon of Winchester's young men often finds itself in Kenilworth's stately parlor. Thaw tolerates their presence but only to a point. When he judges the evening's revelries at an end, he strolls into the room twirling a pistol (rumored to be the one with which he dispatched White) on his index finger. Whistling in a distracted—some would say "insane"—manner, he makes a quick round of the room. Sometimes he makes eye contact with one of his soon-to-be-former guests, eyes bugging in a caricature of the crazy killer. Everyone gets the message, and the room clears noiselessly. Slamming car doors and flying gravel are the usual signals that a Kenilworth social gathering has ended.

What social opportunities are offered to Thaw in Winchester are offered by the Rouss Fire Company, where he soon becomes the most social of its social members. Each Shenandoah Apple Blossom Festival Grand Feature Parade finds him marching in fine fireman's regalia.

The locals grow used to it.

Tourists gawk. Local merchants tell tourists where to find Thaw. Winchester's most infamous resident becomes an attraction on par with the well allegedly dug by George Washington and Stonewall Jackson's former headquarters. When he notices he's being noticed,

Thaw will stare intently at the rube that has stopped to see him.

At times, Thaw's behavior at the fire hall becomes decidedly anti-social. After long nights of poker and drinking, he is known to take target practice at "Old Jake," the six-foot weathervane that tops the turret of the Rouse Fire Hall. A copper creation, Old Jake is a depiction of an early nineteenth-century fireman clutching a bugle with which to call his fellows to action. He fires several shots, always inaccurately, from the pistol that Thaw always has stashed, along with money, in a small leather bag that he keeps close to him at all times in public.

Being unable to hit Old Jake, he turns his marksmanship on street lights and the occasional cat.

Frantic phone calls to find Thaw transportation to Kenilworth always end with Spottswood. Eventually, he is the only one called. (Those who serve as Kenilworth's chauffeur rarely last a week, despite pay well above the local rate.)

The rides with Thaw are always the same.

He is shoved into the back seat, clutching his revolver, which he holds onto with Herculean might. It is always a contest as to which Spottswood will focus on: the light that flashes off the revolver as it passes beneath the street lamps, or the wild eyes—magnified by rimless glasses—of the man who holds it.

The conversation follows the same well-worn path.

"Do you know who I am?"

"Yes, Mr. Thaw."

"Do you know what I did?"

"I was living in New York at the time."

"Under the same circumstances, I'd kill him again, you know."

"Of that I have no doubt."

"I was righteous in what I did. He took my wife's most priceless possession—her virginity. That can't be replaced. A husband has rights in such matters."

"If you say so, sir."

"Have you ever had the urge to kill someone?"

"I served in the war."

"Then you know what it is to kill someone out of righteousness?"

"I can't say that I do."

Silence.

"They say I got away with murder."

"*They* always have a great deal to say."

"Do you think I got away with murder?"

"I am neither judge nor jury."

The barrel of the revolver makes an appearance over the top of the seat.

"I have often thought to test the theory of whether I was spared because of my wealth or the righteousness of my cause."

"How would you do that?"

"I think we both know."

The barrel of the revolver withdraws and philosophical musings of a kind flow from the darkened back seat.

"If I were to take a life again, and I'm not saying I would, I don't think I would shoot someone such as you."

"For that I am thankful."

"Servants, coloreds, colored servants—your lives are not looked upon as meaningful by established society in this part of the country."

"Regretfully, I must agree."

"Still," the barrel of the revolver appears above the back of the seat, "an experiment of such an important nature must begin somewhere."

By this time in the conversation, Kenilworth's driveway is visible.

Spottswood never opens and holds the door as he would for other passengers. He holds the wheel tightly, right foot ready to punch the accelerator should any sudden moves be made in the back seat.

Sometimes, not always, Thaw fires a shot in Spottswood's direction as the cab exits Kenilworth's long driveway. It is a surreal experience—a flash of light followed a split second later by the sound of a shot echoing through the still Shenandoah Valley night. After such occasions, a servant shows up with a discreet brown envelope early the next morning. As he thumbs through its contents, Spottswood thinks of a phrase he heard many years before: "My color is my fortune."

Emma becomes a fixture in the upper echelons of Winchester society, if only discreetly. Her sense of fashion and social etiquette is greatly prized by the grand dames of Washington and Stewart streets, women whose first name becomes "Mrs." upon their marriage. (Obituaries in the *Winchester Evening Star* often list such deceased pillars of society only as "Mrs. William" or "Mrs. John." Emma always feels sorry for such people who readily assign their individuality to oblivion.) Emma knows what colors and cuts will hide the flaws in the figure and that when engraving a silver tray for as a wedding gift, the bride's maiden name is used in the initials.

Emma is always welcome in the finest homes in Winchester but only through the kitchen door.

During the Second World War, gas rationing threatens to doom the Poles Cab Company. Spottswood pulls from his agrarian past to save the business. He contracts with livery men—those familiar with driving carriages are too old to be drafted—to do routine hauling around town. There is even a horse-drawn shuttle to take doctors from the hospital to the country club for Wednesday afternoon golf.

To make grand weddings and funerals possible, Spottswood welds hitches to the front of his cars so that they can be pulled to church by horses. The only time when such economies are not observed is when he drives a serviceman home or takes a minister to tell a family about a loved one who has died in defense of their country.

These occasions always call for the service of a Packard.

There is never a charge to such customers.

The war brings unity of purpose to racially divided Winchester, with one glaring exception. Harold "Howdy" Walker is seen by the African American population and truth be told, in whispered conversations among the whites, as Spottswood's successor as Winchester's greatest athlete. A lithe five feet, eleven inches, 175 pounds, Walker plays all sports well, but none as well as football. He plays for the Brown Bombers, a semi-pro African American team run out of Brown's Barber Shop on the cusp of the rail yard. Technically, Walker is a barber in training, but his main task is playing ball, something he does with rare skill—so rare that all-white Handley High School asks Walker to coach its skill-position players, a blurring of racial lines not seen again until the 1970s.

Whereas Spottswood saw his destiny beyond Winchester, Walker revels in the role of regional hero with no eye to a far horizon. He uses the money he wins in side wagers to buy fine clothes from an itinerant merchant named Irv Shendow, who sets up racks with the latest in New York fashion in an alley behind Miller's Hardware Store on Loudoun Street. Known to be fond of many women, there is one who proves his undoing.

Jessie is a smart, auburn-haired loan clerk at the Farmers & Merchants Bank. She is beautiful in a wholesome way, free-spirited, married, and white. Walker is often seen talking to her at the bank when he has no business there, something noted in heated tones by angry customers behind the closed door of the bank's president.

In 1943, Jessie's husband is a second lieutenant stationed at Fort Meade, Maryland. Refusing to consider the services of Spottswood and other licensed cabbies, Jessie hires Walker to drive her to visit her husband. The drive is long in the days before interstates, much longer than the time Jessie spends with her husband.

Everyone's worst suspicions are realized in early September when a key piece of machinery breaks at the woolen mill on Piccadilly Street, sending the second shift, including Jessie's mother-in-law, with whom she's living, home early. The scream is heard up and down the block when she walks in on Walker and Jessie in bed. The neighbors awoken to their worst fear, Winchester's legal establishment takes decisive action. A Negro in bed with a married white woman—her husband serving his country—is a social abomination that must be dealt with swiftly and decisively.

The shock waves resonate just as deeply in the African American community. When the white sense of decency is deeply wounded, revenge must be taken. With Walker securely locked in the jail on "Potato Hill," any dark face will do when inflicting street justice. African American air raid wardens, supposedly watching for German planes above, instead spend their nights watching the streets for bands of whites seeking vengeance.

White Winchester decides that Walker will be punished swiftly and decisively for his "crime." He is charged with first-degree rape, punishable by death. Also taking a measured approach, the African American community decides it will fight this battle on legal terms. Spottswood attends a meeting at the Black Elks Club on North Kent Street. Its president, Dr. John Paulson, advises those in attendance that their efforts will not be secret long. "I hate to say this, but some colored person is going to carry this news of what we're trying to do back to some white folks' kitchen."

Before the next dawn, Spottswood and Paulson are on the road to meet with an NAACP lawyer in Washington. At the same time, a network of maids, handymen, railroad workers, porters, and other invisible underpinnings of society spread the word that Walker needs money for his defense. The Western Union office at the railway depot dispatches a steady stream of cash to Dr. Paulson from African Americans serving in the military. The NAACP recommends the hiring of Spottswood Robinson, a lawyer in Richmond and one of the few African Americans licensed to practice law in Virginia.

Walker's trial is set a scant three weeks after Jessie's mother-in-law runs screaming into the street. Learning of Robinson's hiring, the trial is moved up a week. A straight razor allegedly taken from Brown's Barber Shop and used by Walker in the "rape" is the only piece of evidence offered to the jury. (The fact that it is shiny and new, as if it had just come out of the package, does not lessen the horror of the all-white, all-male jury.) Walker testifies, although the transcript of his testimony disappears at the conclusion of the trial, never to be seen again. Jessie doesn't testify. The alleged horror of the "crime" committed against her leads her mother to commit her to the state mental hospital in Staunton for the treatment of "nervous exhaustion and hysteria."

The verdict is reached in an hour with the recommendation of the death sentence.

Spottswood is assigned the task of visiting Walker in jail to tell the condemned that his community is gathering money to mount an appeal.

The jail on Potato Hill dates back to the 1840s. Walker and the other African American prisoners are held in a stifling, windowless basement. The walls are painted an aggressive shade of green, paint rejected by the Army repurposed. On this hot, Indian summer night, the newly painted walls, illuminated by light bulbs that work at intervals only they can determine, drip with humidity. Spottswood can't help but think of the Wicked Witch of the West melting as he looks at the walls in Walker's cell.

Walker, stripped to the waist and sweating profusely, leans against the thick, rusted iron bars as he and Spottswood talk. Walker's back is covered by fresh scars. Spottswood, dressed in his Sunday best to convey the gravity of his mission, mops profuse sweat from his face every few seconds.

"They sent you to tell me that I have hope," Walker's tone is cynical.

"Hope is what sustains us."

"Hope is for fools. I had no hope the minute that dumb bitch went screaming into the street."

"We have a good lawyer in Richmond."

"You could have Jesus Christ in a Brooks Brothers suit. There's nothing can save me from electrocution."

"You have to believe—"

"In justice? In God? In what? I'm a Negro found having sex with a married white woman in Virginia. Name me a worse set of circumstances."

"I don't judge."

"You all judge. 'Howdy' went too far. 'Howdy' forgot his place. See what happens when you act on your emotions."

"I don't judge."

"White men have been doing what I did to our women for

centuries. Look around this town. Look at brothers and cousins and sisters and daughters who can't for a moment even think of who they really are."

"I wouldn't know of such things."

"You do know of such things. I've heard the stories."

"This is not about me."

"Not about me either. I'm a symbol. To the whites, I'm a symbol of what happens to Negroes who forget their place. To the Negroes, I'm a symbol of white injustice; even though half of them—and don't you lie—think I'm getting what's coming to me."

"We'll try to help you."

"Too late. Best help yourself by facing the truth."

As he walks down Potato Hill toward home, Spottswood thinks back to Lucy's oft-repeated tale about the man taken off the train in Stephens City.

Virginia executes Walker two weeks later. His body is never returned to Winchester.

Jessie and her husband remain married for three years before discreetly divorcing. Spottswood hears through friends that she lives happily in Baltimore.

Lucy dies in her sleep in March 1947. Spottswood finds his mother in her bed, her face serene and still, everything in the small room laid out in perfect order. Lucy is laid to rest in a grave at Mount Hebron that Major Conrad had purchased more than a half century before through a special dispensation concerning "beloved servants." There is brief consternation among the cemetery board, but after prolonged inspection of Major Conrad's firm penmanship and legal acumen, they can find no justification to deny his wish. Their only restriction on Lucy's funeral is that it be held at a "discreet" time in a "discreet" manner. Spottswood interprets this as a twenty-car procession at one o'clock on a Saturday afternoon.

Certain elements of Winchester society are scandalized.

The year 1947 also brings auspicious news from Brooklyn. Many members of the African American community are near rapture when the Dodgers take the field in April.

Despite the excitement, Spottswood is rarely heard to utter the name Jackie Robinson.

Chapter Thirty-Four

"DID I HEAR..."

CHAUFFEURING PROVIDES the steady income Spottswood needs to pay the day-to-day bills of the cab company. Domestics of all kinds—maids, chauffeurs, cooks, gardeners—are employed by the wealthy and those who wished to appear wealthy of Winchester.

A warm spring afternoon finds Spottswood pulling a chauffeur's cap onto his head as he stands next to his black Packard. The cap completes a well-dressed domestic's uniform of black suit, crisp white shirt, black tie, and shiny black shoes. The car is parked in front of City Hall. As Judge David Simpson, a small, bespectacled man, approaches, Spottswood opens the rear passenger door. After picking up its passenger, the Packard drives through the streets of Winchester.

Judge Simpson grasps the back of the driver's seat and leans forward to talk to Spottswood in a familiar manner. "Do you know someplace where I could get some summer squash for Mrs. Simpson?"

"Mrs. Kirk off Indian Alley has some."

"You know where everything is. It's like you never left Winchester."

"Yes, sir."

"I talked to Mr. O'Connor at the Farmers & Merchants about expanding your cab company. He doesn't usually loan to coloreds, but he was impressed with you and Mrs. Poles, especially Mrs. Poles."

"Thank you, sir. Mrs. Poles has always had a head for business."

"I heard her family had a dry goods business in New York."

"Yes, sir. Mrs. Poles ran her father's haberdashery up in Harlem until the Depression began."

"I'm sure you'll do fine."

Simpson gives the back seat a couple of friendly taps, then sits back. The car drives past a field where a group of boys are playing baseball.

"Spottswood, did I hear that you once played baseball?"

There is a long pause as Spottswood stares straight ahead.

"Yes, sir, I did."

That evening Spottswood walks along the sideline of a game featuring young African American players. An old friend, Raymond Blowe, sticks out his hand, and he and Spottswood talk. When Spottswood walks away, a young ball player, Brooks Lawrence, walks over and talks to Raymond. Brooks is tall, muscular, and very handsome.

"Is that him?"

"Indeed it is," says Raymond.

"What did he say?"

"Nothing much. Never was much of a talker."

"How do I reach him?"

"Never was much of a listener either. Very private, serious man. There is a way to reach him though."

Chapter Thirty-Five

BROOKS

THE NEXT DAY finds Brooks Lawrence on the porch of the Poles home on Fremont Street. The home is small but immaculate. Its bright yellow paint and perfect picket fence stand out from its shabbier neighbors. Brooks, dressed in a suit and tie, knocks on the door. Emma answers, dressed in a floral dress and apron.

"Mrs. Poles?"

"Yes."

"My name is Brooks Lawrence. I play baseball."

"I feel sorry for you."

Brooks looks at Emma's face, then the ground, trying to find a polite way to continue the conversation. He settles on the acknowledgement of her sentiments, followed by the pleading of his case. "Yes, ma'am. I was talking to Mr. Blowe, and he told me Mr. Poles once played baseball in New York."

Emma motions for Brooks to take a seat on a bench on the front porch. She goes into the house and a moment later emerges with a large box. She sits beside Brooks and hands him a picture that Brooks studies for a moment.

"Is that Babe Ruth?"

"Mr. Poles played on his barnstorming tour one year."

"Negroes and whites on the same field?"

"Yes. It wasn't publicized, but yes."

Brooks thinks a bit before asking his next question. "What kind of statistics did he have? Mr. Poles, that is."

"Mr. Poles didn't believe in statistics, with one exception. He always wanted to know what he hit against Satchel Paige. I have statistics from maybe two seasons, that's all."

Brooks is taken aback. "I've never known a player who didn't know all his statistics. How do you measure yourself if not by statistics?"

"Mr. Poles would always measure himself by the reaction of his fellow players. He would say that only someone who played the game could know how difficult it was. If he got a nod or a silent gesture of respect, he knew he'd done well."

"What about the crowd?"

"Fickle. Half of 'em drunk, the other half angry. They were there to take out their frustrations, especially when they were playing on the road. Mr. Poles frustrated fans in many cities that he visited. The respect of his fellow players, especially an opponent—that's what he set his worth by."

"Do you think Mr. Poles could give me some pointers?"

"What position do you play?"

"Pitcher."

"Mr. Poles had little use for pitchers, but I will ask. And what would be the point of his tutelage?"

"Some white boys from these parts, they've signed professional contracts."

"And you're better?"

Brooks looks down for a moment before answering.

"Yes, ma'am."

"And you dream of being a major leaguer?"

Brooks looks down for a long time before answering.

"Yes, I do."

"They say your dreams should be bigger than you are, but sometimes dreams are so big they consume you. Don't let your dreams consume you."

"Yes, ma'am."

"Are you married?"

"No, ma'am."

Emma pats Brooks on the hand. "At least you'll only be frustrating yourself."

"Yes, ma'am." Brooks doesn't know what else to say.

Emma thinks for a moment. "It's best you don't mention this dream to Mr. Poles at present. I will talk to him about what you wish him to do."

That evening's sunset is particularly beautiful. It is the twilight of the gods, the sky turning pink, orange, and purple as Spottswood hits ball after tattered ball from a bucket on the deserted lot that served as his first ball field. He wears the white shirt and black pants of his chauffeur's uniform, suspenders drooping down his backside.

"Did I play ball?"

Emma walks up behind him. "I had someone ask me that today."

Spottswood hits another ball. "So did I," he mutters. "Did I play ball?"

He hits a ball off the rotted remains of the outfield fence, splintering the wood.

"A young man wants your help."

"What good will it do him?"

"What good did it do you?"

"I traveled the world and ended where I started."

Emma turns Spottswood toward her. "It wasn't a wasted trip."

Spottswood turns away from Emma and hits another ball. It lands noiselessly over the fence. He admires his work for a moment. "Show me a man half my age who can hit a ball that far."

"Men half your age could use your help."

Spottswood turns his back on Emma. "Spottswood says no."

"What if Walker had said no to you? Where would you be?"

"Right here hitting baseballs."

"Not if they curved."

Spottswood picks up another ball and hits it.

"Spottswood says no."

"What was it Major Conrad said? 'Never disturb a man at his business.'"

Emma turns and begins walking away, shooting a last word over her shoulder. "What is your business?"

Spottswood drops the bat and walks toward Emma. "You tell me. I don't know any more."

Emma turns to face him. "For years I watched you walk down a road no one wanted you to travel. Lord knows, there were days I didn't want you on that road. The passion you had for baseball frightened me."

"Nothing frightens you."

"Your passion frightens me—has since the day we met. You have to finish the journey. That's all I know for certain. You have to finish. That is your business. Follow your passion to its end."

The next day finds Spottswood striding toward a ball field. Brooks is pitching in a pick-up game between African American players. Spottswood lays his chauffeur's cap on a bench and dons the cap of the New York Elite Giants, which he pulls from his back pocket. He picks up a bat and swings it a few times as he walks to the plate, pushing the batter aside when he reaches his destination. Spottswood digs in and stares Brooks down.

"Never had much use for pitchers."

Spottswood looks at the stunned Brooks.

"Throw!"

Brooks throws a pitch—not his fastest—that Spotts lines into the outfield. "That's what I'd call a 'pity pitch:' something you'd throw to an old-timer you feel sorry for. I said throw the damn ball!"

Brooks throws a curveball that Spotts sends into the outfield. "That wasn't a 'pity pitch,' but it was a pretty pitiful excuse for a curveball. You didn't hide it behind your leg before you went into your windup. Oedipus could have seen that coming."

"Oedipus?"

"Greek guy, played for the Cubs."

"Yes, sir."

Spottswood calls timeout and walks to the mound. "Never, ever call an opponent 'sir.' Never. When you face a man with a bat in his hand, he is trying to steal the food off your plate. If he hits you, you're going to be on the next train home. You have to play with that in mind. You can be as talented as Satchel Paige, but if you don't have some nasty behind your pitch they will eat you alive!"

"Yes, sir."

Spottswood shakes his head. "What did I tell you about 'sir'?" He goes back to the plate and digs in.

Brooks rears back and fires a ferocious fastball that splits the center of the plate belt high. Spottswood watches as the ball hits the catcher's mitt. Brooks looks at Spottswood with a questioning look.

"Think I'll wait on that sorry curveball."

Chapter Thirty-Six

MEMORIAL DAY

IT IS JUNE 6, 1950, Confederate Memorial Day. Spottswood is the lone African American walking among the stream of whites entering the Confederate burial ground in Stonewall Cemetery. Everyone wears their Sunday best. In his arms, Spottswood carries three bouquets of flowers.

The lone car in the procession, a fine convertible, carries an aged woman. A sign on the side of the car bears the legend "Winchester's Last Confederate Widow." People reach out and reverentially touch the car as it passes by.

Appomattox is not recognized within these walls. The glory of the "Lost Cause" lives on in the hope that someday history will be reversed, or at the very least, the current social order maintained.

June 6 is recognized as Memorial Day below the Mason-Dixon Line; the people of Winchester claim they started it. The date is the day of the death of General Turner Ashby, "The Black Knight of the Confederacy" and the cemetery's first prominent resident.

Major Conrad spoke of Ashby, an early leader of the Confederate cavalry, infrequently and in disparaging terms. Though Ashby was a dashing figure who rode a horse of pure black or white, Major Conrad thought he lacked the discipline and foresight needed of a strong commander. (His units were known to run out of ammunition after advancing too far ahead of the main body of troops.)

Ashby was made a general at Winchester's Taylor Hotel, a fine establishment sitting at the center of the town's main street. However, he died but two weeks later, his rank never being confirmed by the Senate in Richmond. Such are the feelings about him that the senators erupt into a prolonged debate about his worthiness for posthumous promotion.

Of such follies are defeat born.

Like his life, Turner Ashby's death was dramatic and reckless.

At the Battle of Good's Farm near Harrisonburg, his horse was shot from under him. Merely inconvenienced, Ashby charged forward on foot, his last words a command and plea: "Charge men! For God's sake, charge!"

He was shot immediately through the heart and died at thirty-three.

There is some debate as to whether the fatal bullet came from the Pennsylvanians before Ashby or his own men behind him. (Major Conrad said, only in the most unguarded of moments, his death probably prevented that of hundreds of men under his command.)

A handsome post-mortem photo of Ashby was taken and reproduced as a sort of holy relic displayed in many prominent Virginia homes.

Originally buried at the University of Virginia cemetery in Charlottesville, Ashby was brought to Winchester to spend his eternal rest next to his brother, Richard. Richard Ashby was bayoneted, allegedly while trying to surrender, in what is now West Virginia (an act recounted over and over to illustrate the demonic nature of the Yankee invaders).

The Brothers Ashby rest under an elaborate tomb next to that of the Brothers Patton.

Spottswood breaks from the crowd and stops at a small plot surrounded by a low stone wall at the edge of the cemetery. He goes inside and places bouquets on the graves of Major Conrad and Tom.

Major Conrad's headstone is large and impressive, standing at the head of columns of Confederate graves like a commander at the head of his troops. All of Major Conrad's achievements and vital dates are listed: Member of the House of Delegates (1860–61); Major 3rd Virginia, CSA (1861–65); State Senator (1875–1890); Solicitor General of the United States (1903–1908).

Tom's headstone is of the small white granite variety found at Arlington Cemetery. It bears the words "Major Tom Conrad, USA, Virginia."

Spottswood pulls some grass from around the base of the tombstones and throws it carefully aside. He bows his head in prayer, not noticing the heated stares shot in his direction. At the end of his prayer, he places flowers on the graves of the Conrads, father and son.

On the other side of Tom's grave is that of Adelaide Hanratty Conrad: "Beloved Mother and Wife." It remains unadorned.

As Spottswood turns and walks away, he is confronted by a middle-aged white man barely suppressing his anger. The red of the man's face stands out against his white suit. A Sons of the Confederacy lapel pin with the stars and bars is the only color on his clothing.

Spottswood doesn't flinch; he looks the man squarely in the eye. "Would you have me lie?" The man gives way as Spottswood moves forward with a purpose.

Spottswood walks outside the wall to one side. There, under a flowering dogwood, is a small, lone headstone with one word,

"Lucy," carved upon it. Spottswood lays down the third bouquet and walks away.

While Howdy Walker's death did not ignite an immediate social rebellion among Winchester's African Americans, it lit a long, smoldering fuse. A local chapter of the NAACP is born and talks about integration continue through the 1950s. The place for meetings is the back of Brown's Barber Shop. As he did in Dixon's parlor, Spottswood assumes the role of listener, and sometimes mediator, as younger men discuss what is and isn't possible in the area of civil rights.

Finally, a white mayor, Claude Smalts, comes up with a unique way to integrate Winchester's business district. Every major store—Sears, J.C. Penney, Woolworth's, Montgomery Ward—will hire one African American sales clerk. Winchester's more bigoted citizens will have to go to another town if they wish to shop. Smalts' plan costs him a nomination to Congress. Spottswood makes sure that anyone needing flowers for a wedding or funeral finds their way to Smalts' Florist shop on National Avenue.

Emma works part-time at Worth's, Winchester's high-couture shopping place for women of taste. Her sense of style is finally appreciated openly.

THE VISITOR

Chapter Thirty-Seven

SPOTTSWOOD DOES MUCH MORE THAN MENTOR BROOKS. He forms the
Poles Cab Company team to showcase Brooks's talent and help
other young men seeking to improve their game beyond the level
of town ball. The team travels the Mid-Atlantic region with more
than a smattering of scouts watching in hopes of finding the next
Jackie Robinson or Larry Doby.

An August evening finds the team warming up before a game in
Chambersburg, Pennsylvania. The field is minor-league caliber with
decent lighting and a large grandstand. The Poles Cab Company
uniforms feature the colors of the New York Elite Giants. Brooks
Lawrence is leading the team through pregame warm-ups as Spottswood watches from the bench. A young white man with flaming
red hair and thick glasses, Bill Veeck, comes up to Spottswood and,
without introduction, sits next to him. Veeck walks with a cane. He
lost his left leg—which has been replaced by a prosthetic—during
World War II.

"Who is that sitting on my bench?" Spottswood asks his unan-
nounced visitor. Veeck sticks out his hand. Spottswood regards it

with disdain for a moment before grasping it.

"Bill Veeck."

"Owner of the St. Louis Browns. Did you not think I know who you are? My question was rhetorical. Every simpleton with half an arm is out there trying to impress you. Of course, every simpleton with half an arm could pitch for the Browns."

"One of them has more than half an arm."

"And more than half a head to go with it. Brooks has too much going for him to pitch for the Browns."

"What, besides his obvious talent, does he have going for him?" Veeck asks.

"Offers from three Negro League teams."

"And they equal the thrill of playing major league baseball?"

"We're still talking about the Browns?" Spottswood raises his eyebrows.

"What's wrong with the Browns?"

"You had a midget playing for you in '51."

"The same year I brought over Satchel Paige."

"I hit him before he turned a hundred."

"He was good enough to go 6–1 with a 2.47 ERA when he helped me win the pennant for the Indians in '48."

"He would have had four times the wins and half the ERA in his prime. Just goes to show how desperate the majors are for talent." Spottswood shakes his head.

"We've got good young talent. We've got Roy Sievers at first, Vic Wertz in right, and Don Larsen on the mound."

"Any midgets?"

"All we need is a few young pitchers like Brooks. The American League has been slow to sign Negroes. You won't see the Yankees here—they won't even consider a Jewish player. Only teams that are willing to explore new sources of talent. Only teams that are willing to do anything to win."

"The last time the Browns won anything was during the war, and that doesn't count," Spottswood remains incredulous. "You had a one-armed man playing for you. When you win with one-armed men, that doesn't count."

"I won in Cleveland, and by God, I'll win in St. Louis if I have to march into hell to find the ballplayers that will make that happen."

"I heard someone say that once. His anger didn't make it happen. Brooks will think about it."

"You know that I—"

"—integrated the American League? What fool doesn't? What you don't say is that you brought up Larry Doby long after the Dodgers had Jackie Robinson on the field. Anyone could see he belonged in your opening-day lineup."

There is a long, awkward silence.

"Your boys play hard," Veeck tries to rekindle some small talk.

"They're men. They play hard because we split the gate 60–40. I don't have to tell you who gets 60."

The awkward silence resumes.

"I heard you were great."

"Still am."

"Who in the majors resembles you?"

"Among the white boys, Musial and Mantle. They stay in their tracks like I did, nice smooth swing, generates smooth power."

"You were as good as Mantle and Musial?"

"Still am when it counts."

The game is about to start. Spottswood pulls his leadoff batter off the on-deck circle and furiously begins swinging a bat. "Take a seat, Pee Wee."

The pitcher on the opposing team gets a disgusted look on his face when Spottswood strides confidently to the plate.

"Sit down, Grandpa!"

"You'll be the only one sitting when I blister your arrogant ass."

"Go back to the rest home!"

"Quit talkin' and bring it to me."

The pitcher gets an angry look on his face and goes into a powerful, full windup before unleashing a sweeping fastball. Spottswood's muscles tense as his fingers play nervously along the bat's handle. Just as he told Veeck, his feet stay in their tracks as the remainder of his body moves in swift, fluid motion. Spottswood catches the ball on the sweet spot, and it rockets through the pitcher's mound up the middle for a base hit. Spottswood chugs to first base before calling for the original leadoff hitter to take his place. He trots back to a position directly in front of Veeck.

"I didn't say I could run like Mantle or Musial. But you wouldn't catch them playing for the Browns. I'm still plenty fast for the St. Louis Browns."

Chapter Thirty-Eight

PAUL

SPOTTSWOOD'S PROFESSION gives him access to the stars that come to Winchester. During the Shenandoah Apple Blossom Festival, he drives Bing Crosby and Bob Hope when they serve as grand marshal. Both men are major league owners (Crosby, the Pirates; Hope, the Indians) and, to Spottswood's gratification, they know who he is.

The Finley Recreation Center on North Kent Street draws a different kind of entertainer—devotees of rhythm and blues or, as some start calling it, rock and roll. The first practitioner of this art form whom Spottswood chauffeurs is "Fats" Domino. When Spottswood hears he'll be driving a hell-raising New Orleans piano player, he almost turns down the job. His opinion changes when he picks "Fats" up at the train station. *If rock and roll is embodied by this chubby youth*, Spottswood thinks, *America's social fabric will not be torn asunder.*

Amazement is a mild description of what Spottswood feels after watching "Fats" attack a piano at Finley's and seeing the reaction of the crowd. "Fats" adds some lyrics to "Blueberry Hill" that he won't sing on *The Ed Sullivan Show*. His rendition of "Junker Blues" shows he's no stranger to the street.

Spottswood's tastes run more to Duke Ellington and Count Basie. Given the polite deference "Fats" gives to Spottswood and Emma, during a brief encounter with her, Spottswood decides to withhold judgment on rock and roll.

Another chauffeuring opportunity materializes in 1953 when Paul Robeson makes an appearance at the Maryland Theatre in Hagerstown. Spottswood finds it odd that he has to drive to Chambersburg, Pennsylvania, to pick Robeson up for an engagement thirty miles away, but remembering the long-ago days in the Dixon parlor, he decides a little extra time with so great a talent will be welcome. Spottswood mentions their past acquaintance soon after picking Robeson up at a surprisingly modest hotel.

"Those days are a long-forgotten dream," the deep voice, touched by weariness, rumbles in the back seat. "Everything was still possible, nothing was out of reach. Now . . ." The voice fades into an awkward, prolonged silence.

After a few miles, Spottswood tries another tactic.

"As you remember, I served with Hamilton Fish during the Great War. He always spoke so highly of you."

"Dear Hamilton," Robeson says, after thinking for a moment. "A great champion of equality and justice, but only if he gets the credit for dispensing them. Twenty-five years in Congress and never once a vote for the working man. Ham Fish fights only for a place in the social register."

After another awkward silence, Robeson restarts the conversation. "I tried to talk Commissioner Landis into letting Negroes into the major leagues. I guess we have that in common."

"Indeed we do."

"It was back in '43. I convinced Landis to let me talk to the owners about breaking the color barrier. With the war and the shortage of able-bodied men, I thought the greedy bastards would at least listen."

"They didn't?" Spottswood already knows the answer.

"No. They did listen. Sat politely, silently. Thing was, Landis told them to ask no questions or engage me in conversation. They sat there like marble busts until I eventually left. I didn't leave right away, though. I wanted them to stew in their cowardice and stupidity for a while."

"You were an incredible athlete. Heard you played baseball."

"Fast too. I'd challenge you to a race, but I feel I'm farther past my prime than you."

"I'd have won."

"I have no doubt you think that you would." Robeson allows himself a small chuckle at this musing.

The brief camaraderie between them is shattered as they arrive at Robeson's destination. Spottswood is aware that Robeson is linked with some politically unpopular causes, but he is not prepared for what he sees outside the Maryland Theatre. A dozen people, all white, march in a circle with placards denouncing Robeson as a communist, a traitor, and un-American.

"Are you sure you want to perform here?" The words escape Spottswood's mouth instinctively.

"God watches over me and guides me. He's with me and lets me fight my own battles and hopes I'll win."

Spottswood knows this has been said many times in reaction to situations such as the one before them. Coming from the back seat in the deep, rich baritone, it sounds biblical.

The Maryland Theatre's dressing room is sparse and amenities few. Spottswood feels apologetic for a wrong he hasn't inflicted as he looks at the bare light bulbs, half burned out, above a cracked mirror. "This isn't a star's dressing room."

"It will do fine for a performer whose options are limited."

"Limited?"

"They've taken away my passport."

"Why?"

"They say I'm a poor representative of America, because I won't denounce Stalin."

"People say he is evil."

"'People' say a lot of things in ignorance. It wasn't until I went to Russia that I saw Negros—Negros who fled this country—treated as equals. For the first time in my life, I walked in full human dignity. Such dignity cannot spring from evil."

The crowd in the thousand-seat theater is disappointing, every cough magnified, every aside, mumbled and otherwise, heard.

During a soliloquy from *Othello*—Robeson is the first African American to play the role on the West End and Broadway—the hostility from the audience reaches a crescendo.

"Speak of me as I am, / Nothing extenuate."

"Commie coon!" The harsh words reverberate through the mezzanine.

"Nor set down aught in malice." Robeson's powerful voice grows in volume. "Then must you speak of one that loved not wisely, / but too well; / Of one not easily jealous, but being wrought—"

"Nigger!"

Pause.

Robeson glares at the audience. He points at the author of this foul epithet. All eyes in the theater fix on a fat, middle-aged white man in the middle rows.

There is silence followed by the loud closing of an exit door as the man leaves.

"Perplexed in the extreme."

The only time when the audience is totally absorbed and silent is when Robeson sings "Ol' Man River" from *Showboat*. Unaccompanied, his rich, full voice bounces off the empty seats and fills the rafters. It is received with the only sustained applause of the evening.

Heading back to Chambersburg, Spottswood looks at Robeson's face in the rearview mirror. Contemplative, sad, defiant, weary—all such states are etched in his countenance. A talent that has performed before kings and queens on Broadway and before audiences of every kind around the world was heckled in a regional theater.

As the car crosses the Mason-Dixon Line into Pennsylvania, a question escapes Spottswood's lips that he feels compelled to ask.

"Why would you put up with that?"

There is silence in the back seat before the answer is offered in that deep, profound voice.

"I'm an American."

Chapter Thirty-Nine

THE INVITATION

FEBRUARY 1954 FINDS Brooks Lawrence in the Poles' parlor saying his goodbyes before departing for the Browns' training camp.

"Don't disgrace us." Spottswood's admonition has the requisite dose of paternalism the occasion calls for.

"Why would he do that?" Emma reflexively straightens the lapels on Brooks's suit.

"Don't get into fights. I won't be there to back you up."

"Not that you'd do him much good."

"Don't be reading Shakespeare around the clubhouse, likely to get your ass kicked."

"Don't use that word!"

"Shakespeare?"

Emma gives a slap to Spottswood's shoulder.

Brooks, dressed in a fine gray suit that Emma picks out with a starched, white shirt and bright red tie, finally finds a place in the conversation. "You toughened up my . . . *behind* . . . to the point it could handle anything."

Emma nervously plays with the handkerchief that pops like a

red rose out of the breast pocket of Brooks's suit. "I don't know if this matches."

"He can wear his underwear on his head if his slider's working."

Knowing the conversation must end so that he can depart, Brooks gathers Spottswood and Emma in his arms.

"If you're struggling out there, remember what I told you about rubbing Vaseline on the ball," Spottswood's advice is muffled by Brooks's embrace.

"Don't have him cheat!"

"Some guys use sandpaper, but if the umpire gets suspicious, you might have to eat the evidence. You don't want to be eating sandpaper."

Brooks makes the St. Louis Browns out of spring training.

On a sunny April morning, Emma hangs up the phone in the Poles' kitchen and sits across the table from Spottswood as they eat breakfast. Each has a plate of food, a cup of coffee, and a newspaper. They wear elaborate silk bathrobes, the last survivors of Dixon's Haberdashery.

Emma reflects for a moment before speaking. "That was Bill Veeck. The Browns are at Griffith Stadium. Brooks is pitching."

Spottswood snaps the paper up in front of him. Emma reaches across the table and gently lowers its top until their eyes meet. "He's sending a car."

Spottswood raises his paper.

"Spottswood says no."

Emma lowers the paper again.

"A major league owner is sending a car for you."

Spottswood raises the paper again.

"The Browns still in the majors? Says here they're in eighth place. Only reason they're not in ninth is there's only eight teams in the league. Senators aren't much better. Only thing keeping them out of the cellar is the Browns. Bunch of bush leaguers."

Emma lowers the paper.

"A major league owner is sending a car for you."

Spottswood snaps the newspaper up.

"I have eight cars, all V-8s. Got my name painted on the side. If I want to go to Washington, I'll find the keys. Spottswood says no."

Emma yanks down the paper with a force that splatters the food as it hits the plate.

"Emma says yes!"

Emma snaps her paper up. After a look of amazement leaves his face, Spottswood tentatively lowers her paper.

"Do you know what kind of riff-raff hangs around the ballpark?"

Emma gives a look of mock amazement and snaps her paper back into place.

"What time are we leaving?"

Chapter Forty

RENEWED ACQUAINTANCE

LATER THAT DAY, a chauffeured black Cadillac pulls up outside the players' entrance at Griffith Stadium. Veeck meets the car, opens the door, and helps Emma get out. Spottswood gets out the opposite side.

"We're hitting in the top of the first."

"That shouldn't take long." Spottswood's aside drips with disdain.

Veeck leads Spottswood and Emma into the stadium's substructure, nodding at the guard at the gate who is surprised at the sight of a woman entering baseball's sacred confines. After walking through a long, dank tunnel, the sign "Visitors' Locker Room" is illuminated by a single light bulb above the door. Veeck motions for Emma to stay at a discreet distance as he opens the door and checks inside.

"Let me make sure it's clear."

Veeck opens the door. He and Spottswood go in. Street clothes hang in the back of lockers that uniforms hung on a couple of hours before. Half-empty coffee cups and unfolded newspapers litter a communal table at the room's center.

As Veeck goes ahead to search through the locker room, Spotts-wood's eyes are caught by a long, lean figure sitting recumbent in front of a locker. Satchel Paige is smoking a cigarette. His uniform shirt is unbuttoned to the waist, revealing an old T-shirt underneath.

"Still taking care of your health?" Spottswood's voice startles Paige, who quickly recovers his ever-present cool.

"Way these guys hit, I could pitch on one leg."

Spottswood contemplates the image before him for a long moment. "You made it."

"Said I would. You—"

"I had my day."

Paige snuffs out his cigarette.

"I know."

Veeck crosses behind Spottswood on his way back to the locker room door. There is a long silence.

"Seeing you pitch makes me want to grab a bat."

"You never could hit me. What did you hit against me?"

Emma noiselessly comes to Spottswood's side.

"411." The feminine voice startles a clubhouse attendant who has begun cleaning up.

Paige gets up and gives Emma an affectionate hug. Spottswood pulls Emma away when Paige's arms linger a bit too long and firmly pushes the pitcher away.

Paige looks at Emma approvingly. "Field hand, it's a good thing you have somebody to do your ciphering." He glances disdainfully at Spottswood. "The finest-looking woman Harlem ever produced with you. There is no justice in this world."

Paige walks across the locker room, buttoning and tucking his shirt in as he goes, his back to Spottswood and Emma. The shirt buttoned and in place, Paige places his cap on his head and adjusts it.

He then turns, looking every inch a major leaguer. Paige touches his heart before raising his arm and pointing at Spottswood: "I know."

Paige goes into the tunnel to the dugout, his cleats echoing on its concrete. As if drawn by a sound of a distant drum, Spottswood follows, Emma several steps behind.

The tunnel is dark, save for a few dim light bulbs that cast an uncertain yellow light. At the end of the tunnel is the bright light reflected off the field. Spottswood moves through shadows and into the light.

Spottswood looks out on the field where Brooks Lawrence is pitching. The scoreboard behind him shows the count is three and two. Emma comes up behind Spottswood.

"I hope he doesn't throw a curveball behind in the count."

"He has confidence in it."

"Don't throw the curveball."

Emma has spoken a bit too loudly, and the eyes of the Browns turn toward the sound of a female voice. Spottswood looks at Emma. "Never disturb a man at his business."

On the mound, Brooks rears back and throws a wicked curveball. The catcher's mitt pops as the batter swings and misses. The catcher throws the ball to third base. The Browns are going around the horn after a strikeout. When the ball reaches Roy Sievers, the white first baseman, he trots to the mound and puts it in Brooks's glove before giving him a hearty pat on the back.

Emma and Spottswood reach for each other's hand and grasp them tightly.

EPILOGUE

SPOTTSWOOD POLES DIES ON SEPTEMBER 2, 1962.

They find him in his favorite chair in the house on Fremont Street, a copy of the *Sporting News* on his lap. He lives long enough to see African American stars, many of whom go to the Hall of Fame, dominate the game he dominated.

Emma sells the cab company in 1963 but not before using all of its vehicles to transport people to the March on Washington. She hears Dr. Martin Luther King Jr. speak the words she harbors in her heart from the steps of the Lincoln Memorial.

With her profits from the cab company, Emma buys Worth's, which she operates successfully until her death in 1968. Spottswood and his beloved wife are buried in Arlington National Cemetery.

Spottswood Poles is nominated numerous times for the Baseball Hall of Fame but lacks the statistical validation to be elected.

There is no plaque in Cooperstown honoring him, which might be just as well.

Legends are cast on the wind and in the heart, not in bronze.

Wayde Byard

ABOUT THE AUTHOR

WAYDE BYARD HAS LIVED TWO LIFETIMES: one as an award-winning journalist, the other as a public relations professional for one of America's largest school systems. A graduate of the University of Missouri's famed School of Journalism, Wayde has served as a crime reporter, government reporter (there are those who would say crime and government are related), sports editor, and Associated Press College Basketball Pollster. It was on a rainy summer day that he first discovered Spottswood Poles in the basement archives of Winchester, Virginia's Handley Library. In the more than two decades since, Wayde has told Poles's story in a screenplay that has won state and national awards. Although he has interviewed more than fifty members of the Baseball Hall of Fame, Wayde knows that Poles's story is still the one that resonates most deeply in his soul.

When not writing, Wayde is known to thousands of easily impressed children (and their more easily impressed parents) as the guy who makes snow day calls. This has resulted in several undeserved public service awards that he cherishes nonetheless.